SO MANY LIVES

AND ALL OF

THEM ARE YOURS

SO MANY LIVES

AND ALL OF

THEM ARE YOURS

RON BUTLIN

Polygon

First published in hardback in Great Britain in 2023
by Polygon, an imprint of Birlinn Ltd.

Birlinn Ltd
West Newington House
10 Newington Road
Edinburgh
EH9 1QS

9 8 7 6 5 4 3 2 1

www.polygonbooks.co.uk

ISBN 978 1 84697 631 5
EBOOK ISBN 978 1 78885 582 2

British Library Cataloguing-in-Publication Data
A catalogue record for this book is available on
request from the British Library.

Typeset in Sabon LT Pro by The Foundry, Edinburgh
Printed and bound in Great Britain by Clays Ltd, Elcograf S.p.A.

For my good friends Margie Aikman, Steve Catterall, Lynda Clark, Richard Mowe as well as my sister Pam Thomson and my wife Regi Claire

PART ONE

SATURDAY

It is almost midnight when Morris begins his descent into the village. With no moon and only a scattering of stars above, it feels like he's about to land on a dark and unknown planet.

At the foot of the hill he pulls up, cuts the engine and starts to breathe once more. These days, two hours' driving at night is two hours too many.

As if it was marked with an X, he has parked on the very spot where he saw his father for the last time, shaking his fist at him. It's tempting to run the car back and forth over the stretch of gravel and grind that particular memory into the dirt. But he won't. Coming here, Morris reminds himself, is his chance to finally let go of the bad stuff.

The cold already beginning to seep in, he takes his coat, document case and holdall from the passenger seat and climbs stiffly out the car. He has arrived – safe, sound and sober.

He starts towards the cottage. As a small boy he boasted that he lived in the only back-to-front house in the whole of Scotland, a very special house whose front door and windows faced the garden and whose back wall faced the street. Same as all those years ago the garden gate gives an unoiled screech as he pushes it open. A welcome, of sorts. He follows the cement path round to the front and lets himself in.

It's colder inside than out. He fumbles for a light switch, then remembers – no electricity. The torch on his mobile shows him a kitchen that's lost the will to live. No cooker, no fridge, wrecked sink unit, cupboard with no door; the walls a Jackson Pollock of damp stains and mould; the floor more cement than linoleum. A bit on the grim side, but he's not planning to entertain.

The estate agent told him the electricity had been disconnected at source. No problem, but with his phone battery near-zero he'll need to move fast.

She mentioned . . . something . . . in the sink unit. A *drawer* where there might be . . .

Where there *are*. Candles. Matches, too. Thank fuck.

The first two matches leave a red smear on the box; the third flares. He lights a candle and locates the electricity meter. Luckily it's nearly as ancient as he is. He melts the candle base, plants it on top to help him see better, then lays out the tools he has brought with him from Edinburgh: pliers, scissors, insulating tape and a magnet. Now for the tricky bit. Like Kyle had shown him all those lifetimes ago back in London, he tracks the wires connecting the meter to the outside supply and starts snipping what needs snipped, splicing what needs spliced and bypassing what needs bypassed. Too many wires, of course, but he picks the right ones. He hopes.

He flicks the big red switch and the kitchen light snaps on; a reassuring hum comes from the meter. Now for his magnet. The cost-saving beauty is slapped into place, and job done. Things are looking good. He plugs in his mobile to charge.

The water?

On with both taps at once. Not a fucking drop. Either it's been turned off at the mains or else it's in the pipes and still frozen, which doesn't bear thinking about. He'll go with *turned off*.

The stopcock is just beside the front door. After a few pipe-rattling coughs the rusty-looking gushes begin running clear. Thank fuck once again. At a sudden gurgling from inside the cupboard he steps over to check and . . . *Halleluiah!* He'll soon have a boiler full of hot water. Central heating even, maybe.

Out with his camping stove and small saucepan, and on with water for tea. Things are looking even better. He'll have time for a quick look round. Like a long-ago miner exploring an abandoned mine, he sets off, candle in hand, dripping melted wax as he goes.

Turns out there are no bulbs in any of the other rooms, no central heating either. His childhood bedroom, just off the kitchen, has most of its ceiling lying on the floor. The sitting room, the middle room of the cottage, looks like a building site. Next is the small bathroom – a swift peek is enough. His parents' old bedroom at the far end is another building site, but worse. A bomb crater more like. He pauses in the doorway. This, he reminds himself, is the room where he was born. After a final glance round, he pulls the door shut.

Back in the kitchen, the water's coming to the boil. With his sleeve, he wipes the draining board clear of dead flies and mouse-shit, then upends his goodybag: tins of ravioli, peas, Scotch broth, frankfurters; half a packet of Coco Pops, an individual pork pie, teabags and some sachets of Cup-a-Soup. He forgot the bread and can picture the milk and butter still sitting in his fridge back home. Having reached the no-wine and no-brandy at the bottom, he scrunches up the empty bag and drop-kicks it across the kitchen.

The camping stove switched off, he reaches for—

No mug. He forgot that as well. Remembered a knife, fork and spoon, at least.

Under the sink he finds more dead flies, cobwebs, rags, old crockery, a few slates and a dented metal bucket. Mouse-shit over everything like a topping of hundreds and thousands. Then . . . no handle, but it'll do.

A swirl-out under the tap, in with a teabag and, not a moment too soon, he clasps his hands round the mug for warmth. The pork pie is gone in seconds.

Ping, ping, ping, ping. A rush of texts from his daughter Elise and son Tom, known affectionately as the Accusations. *Arrived okay, Dad? Are you okay, Dad? Call me. Call me. Dad? Let's hear from you! Pleeeeeease.*

He'd been in such a rush to get out of Edinburgh that he didn't tell them until he'd left his flat, texting while going down the stairs. His mobile rang within seconds.

It was Elise, shocked that he hadn't talked things through with them. Tom's text came moments later. Hoping to keep things short, he carried on down, out into the street and into his car where he sat behind the wheel, going nowhere. More calls, more texts. Finally it was settled he would message them both last thing every night to confirm he was safe and well. But, as he stands here in this half-demolished kitchen, he is pleased they have ignored what was agreed, pleased almost to the point of tears. He knows he should count himself lucky. Correction: he *does*. His children really care.

Fuck. Because, like a bad taste in his mouth that he's never had the courage to spit out, here comes the real question: Tom and Elise care, but does *he*? They are anxious to know if their dad's all right. Well, is he? He starts to text back:

– *Thanks, Tom, Thanks, Elise. All's well. I'm fine. Everything's fine . . .*

Then he pauses. Planning to stay alone in a derelict cottage with no heating, no furniture and only one lightbulb, and their seventy-year-old dad thinks he is *fine*? Really?

He carries on:

– *Getting settled in now and off to bed soon. Thanks for all your texts. Please don't worry. Sleep well. Night-night!* He adds a triple thumbs-up, two hearts, a few XXXs, and signs off: *Love you, Dad.* Because he does. Of course he does. Loving *them* is not the problem. He taps Send and quickly powers down.

Really tired all at once, he goes outside for an al fresco

pee in the dark and a look at more stars than he has seen in years. Living in the city, he has forgotten what a glorious sight they are. He starts to count them, and the more he counts the more there seem to be, which feels strangely reassuring. Zip up, then back into the kitchen. As the only lightbulb in the cottage is set too high to be unscrewed, he takes a chipped soup plate from under the sink for his candle. He sticks a second candle beside it, and then a third. A three-branch candelabra, Scottish-style.

Into the sitting room. Light a fire, or go straight to bed? No contest. He tosses aside the broken bricks, lumps of solid plaster and torn cement sacks, then unrolls his sleeping bag along the back wall. His holdall will do as a pillow. The estate agent would be shocked. He can still hear the bewilderment in her voice. *There's no bed, Mr Magellan. Are you going to sleep on the floor?*

Shoes kicked off, he sets a new record for sliding into a sleeping bag fully dressed, then pulls his coat on top for a quilt. He reaches for his life-support system – his iPod and buds – and settles for Haydn's Symphony No. 4, the *andante*. Hardly into the first repeat, he buttons it off. Too tired, even to be soothed. His candelabra's snuffed out with a wet thumb – *pssst, pssst, pssst*. He snuggles down, closes his eyes . . . and, ever so gradually, starts to warm up.

There's a *drip-splat, drip-splat, drip drip drip . . .* coming through the wall from the bathroom. A leak, but it doesn't sound too bad. Its steady rhythm is almost comforting. He'll deal with it tomorrow. A final thought before drifting off to sleep: returning here to the cottage after circumnavigating his threescore and ten, he really has come full circle. He is ready to kickstart his life all over again – and this time get it right.

*

Your childhood lasted for two days only: Day One, which was whenever your father was at home; and Day Two, whenever he wasn't. Of Day One you remember only the fear. Day Two came with a soundtrack – your mother playing her piano. On Day Three you left.

Waking early on your sixteenth birthday you threw off the bedcovers and rushed across to the window. Blue skies, bright sunshine flooding the garden and not a sign of rain – you couldn't have planned it better. You dressed quickly, shouldered your backpack and tiptoed out of your bedroom. Only to find your mother waiting in the kitchen. The two of you had to speak in whispers. She was in tears as she hugged you and wished you a happy birthday, slipping you a five-pound note. She gave you the pack of sandwiches she had made the night before.

After one last hug you set off to walk the three miles to the main road. At the top of the steep hill leading out of the village you glanced back – and there she stood, a small hunched figure at the garden gate. You waved to her. There was no response at first. Couldn't she see you? You waved again, both arms sweeping side to side above your head. Finally she raised her hand. After one last goodbye wave you continued on past the schoolmaster's house, Langside farm and the church. Soon you were striding out at a good firm pace. It was a fine September morning and ham sandwiches had never tasted better.

Ten hours and nearly a dozen lorries and vans later you arrived in London. Dropped off somewhere on the North Circular, you wandered around for several hours before unrolling your sleeping bag in a park, Ealing Common. Luckily it wasn't raining. You were so exhausted that the traffic rumbling past all night soothed you; sirens tore into your sleep but for hardly more than a few seconds each time. You learnt a basic truth: the real cold comes from underneath. It was five a.m. and still dark when you woke up, shivering from head to toe.

Guided by the immense signpost at the Hanger Lane junction, you took what you hoped would be the most direct route into the city centre, walking fast to defrost yourself on the way. As it began to get light you stopped for breakfast at a tea stand in Shepherd's Bush. After sixteen years in your grim, rain-sodden Scottish village you could only stand and gape. Here was real life, here was excitement! Mug of tea in one hand and bacon roll in the other, you looked on as black guys, white guys, turbaned Sikhs and women in brightly coloured saris and shawls assembled the open-air market to a sound-mix of boom-box reggae, ragas and The Beatles. By the time you finished bacon roll number two, the metal struts on the nearest stall had been slotted and bolted into place. Your second tea saw lengths of canvas being unrolled and tied in position; T-shirts and jeans were being unpacked and stacked on trestle tables, ready for business. Your village now seemed on a faraway and very dull planet.

Your meal over, the road into the city centre continued more or less straight and, as the sun rose above Notting Hill Gate, you became invisible.

From then on, every day was the same day over, a day that soon became longer and lonelier than any you had ever known before. No one looked at you, no one spoke to you. You trekked the same streets, slumped down onto the same benches, sheltered in the same alleys and doorways. There were vast buildings, monuments and statues everywhere you looked. While Nelson turned a blind eye, you made your way round and round Trafalgar Square learning how to beg. You gazed into steamed-up café windows, and ate in the street. Hamburger rolls, hot dogs, or nothing. You were chased out of Underground stations, out of warm and crowded arcades, Oxford Street stores. Along the railings at Piccadilly Circus, you saw a line of teenage boys, younger than you even, some of them. T-shirt, jeans, duffel bag. Looking for a meal, a bed for the night. Looking for cash.

Wardour Street, Soho Square, Shaftesbury Avenue. Charing Cross Road, The Strand, Bond Street, Oxford Circus. You were looking for – what? You didn't know and had no one to tell you. There were whole days when you didn't speak apart from mumbling: 'Can you spare me . . .?' which said it all. You walked and walked, trudged and trudged.

You quickly learned three further basic truths:

Look too wretched – and the response will be disgust, not cash.

Not eating for two days means you stop feeling hungry.

There are predators. Always.

When the sun began sliding from the sky, you hunted for shelter. So much glass, steel and concrete, so many lighted windows. So many locked doors.

No stars shone above this city; church bells rang out the hours, but not for you. A tide of traffic and pedestrians flowed in each morning and ebbed away each evening, leaving you marooned and utterly alone. Weather was everything. When it was wet, you stayed wet. Cold, you stayed cold. Keeping warm and dry took the whole day. You ate well, or not at all. The same day was trekked up and down a hundred times. After a week, a fortnight, it was still the same day. Washing in public toilets, sleeping on benches, in church crypts, railway stations, bus stations, cemeteries. Getting moved on, and getting moved on.

There was angel dust, grass, bombers, reds, but you preferred music, the music you carried in your head. You carried it always, and still do. Beethoven's vigour and drive gave you the energy to keep going; a Chopin nocturne consoled you as you fell asleep under a bridge or in a park or a basement yard. You remembered Day Two, your mother playing her piano. Music.

Unlike everything else in your life, it always made sense.

Late one afternoon you were working your way round the tourists in Leicester Square when you felt a hand on your shoulder.

'You look like you're not going to make it.'

The hand guided you over to a bench. The couple sitting there abruptly got to their feet and disappeared. You sat, but didn't speak. What was there to say? A few years older than you, taller, broader, long dark hair and a full beard. He asked your name and how long you had been in London. When did you last eat? While he talked, you realised you were holding back tears. He wrote down an address.

'It's called Middle Earth. Kind of a crash pad / fuck pad for friendly hobbits.' He gave you a bar of chocolate and bus fare. 'Ask for Kyle, and say Big Frodo sent you.'

This was your first bus ride in London and so restful that you fell asleep, nearly missing your stop. The Sikh conductor remembered for you. Getting out near the Acton Town tube station, you asked directions until you found the street. It was a long line of terraced houses, with parked cars in front and gardens that were mostly cement, dustbins and lace-curtained windows. A fuck pad around here? At worst, you could doss down out of sight in one of the small basement yards.

The street ahead sweeping round in a slow curve, you saw a house with its windows boarded up. As you approached the front gate, you heard someone picking out Dylan on a guitar.

Given a bowl of soup and a stretch of floor, you and your sleeping bag slept round the clock. There was always soup on the go at Middle Earth. Melody and the other 'chicks' did the rounds, wafting into the local shops on clouds of patchouli and dope, and wafting back out with bones, bacon scraps, bruised fruit and yesterday's bread. Melody also organised the cooking on a lethal-looking pre-war electric cooker. The scavenged food was bulked out with brown rice, lentils or pulses, depending on the meal's Ying/Yang status.

After the streets, Middle Earth was luxury. The electricity had been reconnected and a strong magnet fitted to the meter so the revolving disc that measured usage was forced to turn with glacial slowness. There was even a phone, though it had to be reconnected to the junction box every time, and – same as making free calls from a public box – the number wasn't dialled but tapped out on the cradle. It didn't receive incoming calls.

'We're gypsies . . .' Kyle, the squat's supremo, sat cross-legged on the floor firing up the morning joint, '. . . urban nomads travelling from oasis to oasis, without the need to lug around tents and carpets. We are not possessed by our possessions.' Having taken the first hit, he handed the joint to one of his acolytes, picked up a Golden Virginia tin and set about crafting the follow-up. Rizla papers were stuck together and the extended furrow sown with tobacco. A generous sprinkling of dope was crumbled on top and then, in an effortlessly smooth motion, he rolled, licked and pressed the joint into its bloated and cheerful cigar shape.

'This place . . .' he continued as he slid a homemade filter of rolled-up cardboard into one end, '. . . is an inheritance, a family dispute that's got bogged down with lawyers. We have an understanding with them, sort of.' He paused to twist the other end tight, ready to be lit. 'We're doing everyone a favour. With us here, the place won't get broken into, won't get trashed by drunks and dossers.' A match put to the twisted end, he sucked in deep and *held* . . . After several very long seconds the smoke came trickling out on a sigh of satisfaction.

'Everyone contributes, Melody and the other chicks included. "Each according to his means", as the great man said.'

'I could always help keep the place tidy,' you suggested, 'wash the dishes and hoover—'

'Already done.'

Really? The unswept floor crunched underfoot and every surface felt sticky. The toilet – in a small shed out back – needed flushed each time with a pail of water.

'But I could—'

The supremo raised his hand for silence. 'Hard cash.' He gave a maharishi smile. 'For life's little extras, for rainy days.'

You offered a joke. 'For our old age?'

'Old age? We're living *now*, man, and always will. There is nothing else. No past, no future. Only the *now* exists. This . . .' Kyle rapped his knuckles on the floorboard, '. . . is *maya*. Illusion.' He took another hit from the joint, held it for several seconds, then let it go. 'Hard cash. Third of what you earn goes into the kitty and the rest is yours to keep. No rush. You need to get your strength back, your spirit needs time to heal.' Then came the punchline. 'When you can feel your sweet young blood flowing once more in your veins . . .'

Your sweet young blood? You pictured the rent boys at Piccadilly Circus.

*

Jerked abruptly out of sleep, Morris lies wide awake, rigid, holding his breath. *Something* woke him. He strains to hear the sounds of – the creak of a floorboard? A door handle being turned? *Drip-splat, drip-splat, drip, drip—*

It would make sense to light the candle, but . . .

He remains rigid, fists clenched tight at his sides. Listening, listening. Is this him straight back to Day One, straight back to listening outside the sitting room door, trying to guess what kind of mood his father was in?

Thud. From through in the kitchen. Something solid?

Matches, candle. He eases himself out of the sleeping bag, tiptoes across to the kitchen door and throws it open, snapping on the light in time to glimpse a brown-black dart of speed shoot off the draining board and disappear under the sink with a flick of its tail.

He is so relieved, he almost laughs out loud. *That* was his terrifying father? A ghost with four paws and whiskers!

The tin of Scotch broth is lying on the floor; there are teeth-marks in the packet of ginger snaps, and a bitten-into sachet of Cup-a-Soup has leaked into a small heap of droppings. He tosses everything bar the tin of soup into the metal bucket and covers it with a couple of slates. An instant larder, mouse-proof.

Back in bed, he is on the point of falling asleep again when something occurs to him. Something so obvious and yet he can't quite grasp its significance. *His father?* The fact is, he is now older than his father will ever be.

Woken by the morning sun, Morris snuggles down deeper into the sleeping-bag warmth. By daylight the sitting room looks grimmer than ever. Bare floorboards, wallpaper hanging in strips, patches of exposed lath and plaster, rubble everywhere and a fireplace choked with soot. Anyone glancing in would take him for a dosser.

Dosser? They couldn't be more wrong. He's been there, done it and got the scars to prove it. Same with the big salary, the family and the suburban dream. Ancient history. From now on, he is going to make every moment count. This morning and every morning he will get up early. He will shower, shave, get dressed, light a fire, have breakfast. Then he will work. And work. And work. He has several wasted lifetimes to put firmly behind him.

Still clutching his sleeping bag up to his chin, he gets to his feet. He hesitates . . . Then, like someone who has been taking part in a sack race, he drops the bag to the floor, steps into his shoes, grabs clean clothes and a towel from his holdall and hurries through to the bathroom.

Only to stop in the open doorway. If last night's candlelight was discouraging, daylight is stark and unforgiving. He can see now that the floor has been lifted, leaving only the bare joists. When touched even lightly, the wash-hand basin wobbles on its free-standing pipework; the lidless and seatless WC trickles indifferently into its bowl; the shower-tray is a super-sized Petri dish of yellow, green and blue mould into which the rusted showerhead continues to mark time with its *drip-splat, drip-splat, drip, drip, drip* . . .

Ex-wife Mary would have the whole lot gutted and IKEA-ed in time for lunch. He'll let it live. He revises his schedule. Forget showering. After a pee in the pan followed by a splash at the sink while touching as few surfaces as possible, he leaves. The day ahead is a flatpack with no instructions, except that he is here to work, work, work.

Putting on his coat, he goes through to the kitchen and gets breakfast out of the bucket. He eats standing up: a mug of black tea, bread, butter and handfuls of crunchy-dry Coco Pops.

Because yesterday's unexpected phone call had come early in the morning, Morris missed most of it.

'Morris Magellan, the composer?'

'What? I . . .' He had been deeply asleep.

'My name is McGibbon . . . been let down . . . very last minute . . . for string quartet.'

'String quartet?'

'No *squeaky gate* stuff . . . a good tune. Stravinsky's best was neo-classical, remember . . . agreement . . . email . . .'

Call finished, Morris had drifted back to sleep.

Surfacing around midday, he remembered having had a really strange dream about a phone call where someone had actually . . . A commission to write a string quartet? If only. He forgot all about it, and not until his four o'clock jingle-break for tea and a Snowball did he get round to checking his emails.

He stared at the screen. Was he still dreaming? If so, the dream was pretty vivid and came complete with a PDF attachment – a two-page 'informal agreement' in numbered paragraphs. The bold type in paragraph five insisted there was to be no *squeaky gate* music, explaining, within square brackets, that what was needed were bums on seats and *Likes* on social media. Paragraph six was brief: length to be ten minutes max, 'max' in bold and underlined.

Clearly some kind of mistake had been made if McGibbon thought he was a real composer who composed real music for real musicians. Morris had been about to email the man back to clarify the situation when . . .

A string quartet? Well, he was a sort of composer, wasn't he?

He had glanced up from his Snowball in time to see Beethoven staring down at him from his poster above the fridge. Morris could almost hear Ludwig's thick

Bonn accent: *The man wants a quartet, so give him a quartet.* This, from the composer who sometimes sold the same composition several times over to different publishers. So why not?

For starters, he might get found out. But as no fee had been mentioned there would be no fraud, no *financial* fraud, at least. And, after all, the man had come to him, sent him a contract.

He had been about to bite into his Snowball when Beethoven urged him a second time: *Don't think about it. Thinking is overrated.* Snowball in hand, Morris considered the pros and cons. Was he afraid he might not be able to deliver? He might, he might not – but behind the artistic doubts loomed the real question. Would he rather be:

A. A drunk churning out slot machine jingles?

or

B. A real composer creating real music?

He put down his Snowball. Many musicians consider the string quartet the purest form of all. Such masterpieces as those of Haydn, Beethoven, Mozart, Bartók, Shostakovitch. He glanced up at Beethoven. The great composer had lived his life and now Morris had to live *his*. But a life dedicated to writing jingles for slot machines to keep himself in wine and brandy? Anyway, what did he have to lose – his reputation?

Put like that, it was a no-brainer. In his old life he'd have cracked open a new bottle of Courvoisier to celebrate, but not any more. His old life was history and his real life just beginning. From the instant he emailed McGibbon back, agreeing to everything, he felt a surge of energy he hadn't known in ages. Like he'd been locked up all his life, and was setting himself free. Being reborn, but even better.

Real music would need real inspiration. He had to get away from the city, away from the scenes of . . . *failure*. He began scouring the net. Like a sixties' rock band, he needed to find somewhere in the country where he could get it together and tune in to his true creativity. It would have to be cheap, of course, something basic, something . . .

Morris recognised the cottage straightaway. It was for sale, and quite definitely wasn't selling. After some pleading and haggling on the phone, a month's 'holiday' let was agreed. The keys were couriered over. He knocked off the jingle-in-progress in record time, ordered a chow mein special online, and then packed. His endless discussion with the Accusations over, it had been after ten when he drove off through the empty streets and out of the city. He was doing what he should have done a long time ago. And it felt great.

For inspiration, Beethoven would sometimes walk in the fields and woods of the Viennese countryside. But on this, his first morning as a real composer, Morris is so keen to get down to work that he settles for a few inspiring lungfuls of fresh air on the cottage doorstep. His mug of tea raised in a toast to new beginnings, he glances over to . . .

Fuck's sake, where the hell are the fruit trees? What's

happened to the lawn? When he arrived last night it had been too dark to see anything, but he is seeing it now, and seeing it big time – most of the garden's been annexed by a glass-and-brick newbuild with double parking out front. A fence cuts the lawn in half and a black SUV squats just beyond it like the tank of an occupying army. All within spitting distance.

On the plus side, his parents' old garage is still standing and so is the storeroom next to it. But even so . . . The small four-tree orchard has been cut down, and the rows of his mother's green beans, potatoes, carrots and strawberries tarmacked over. It's all *wrong*, is the best he can come up with. It looks wrong and feels wrong.

He is still staring at the newbuild, and staring hard, when the front door opens and a youngish-looking man marches out, carrying a large cardboard box. Red puffer jacket topped by a red face and red baseball cap like he is coming to the boil from the waist up. He is clearly in a hurry, but takes care as he sets down his box on the SUV bonnet. Noticing Morris, he gives a wave. To forestall any possibility of his quartet getting delayed by hello-neighbour banter, Morris gives him a quick wave back and retreats, pulling the door firmly shut. Through the kitchen window he watches the friendly puffer stow his box in the car and go back inside his house.

He is supposed to be working, Morris reminds himself. This is the first day in his life as a real composer writing real music for real—

Puffer appears with another box that has something green sticking out of the top. A plant?

Morris forces himself to turn away. Beethoven didn't spend his time looking out the window, goggling the neighbours. Beethoven got on with writing his string quartets.

The sitting room feels even colder than when he arrived. Work in here and he risks pneumonia. He needs a fire. Down on his knees, he scoops the soot out from the grate, tears a cement sack into strips that he scrunches into tight balls. Some sticks on top for kindling? Plenty smashed brickwork but no wood. Pull out a few exposed laths? One good tug . . . but he might start an avalanche of dust and rubble, and bring down the whole wall. The discarded floorboards in his parents' old bedroom looked good and solid, and will give out a grand heat. They'll never be missed. He returns, trailing a six-foot length of floorboard behind him. Too big for the grate, of course, so he angles it against the wall and tries to stomp it in half. Which nearly breaks his leg. Maybe there is an old saw or axe lying around somewhere?

Outside, he finds the door of the storeroom – where tools and garden stuff used to be kept – locked, and with not a millimetre's give. No key in the kitchen drawer, no key anywhere. A locked door standing between him and getting started on his quartet? Beethoven would kick it in while whistling *Ode to Joy*. By now Mr Newbuild over the fence is probably at one of the windows, eye-balling his every move. And so . . .

Counting one . . . two . . . three . . . four . . . five . . .

Morris squints down at the lock, then gazes up like he's trying to remember something. Time for the pantomime slap on the forehead: *of course!* He dashes indoors, and is back out a moment later, flourishing the front-door key – and not-flourishing the rusty chisel he had noticed among the junk under the sink. Seconds later the storeroom door swings open.

Stone floor, stone walls, windowless and always freezing in winter, this was where the coalman emptied his huge sacks into one corner and the forestry man his logs in another.

*

It had been the evening before your sixteenth birthday. A trailer-load of logs delivered earlier that day needed chopping. This was one of your favourite jobs and you always enjoyed yourself, singing out loud as you swung the axe, bringing it down hard on the beat to split the wood with a *crack*.

Having upended an oversized log on the chopping block, you had been about to raise the—

'Useless. Might have known you'd not be doing it right. You're a waste of space.' You hadn't heard your father come into the storeroom. 'Give me the axe!'

One day more, and you might have done just that.

*

Morris switches on the light and—

And he has floodlit the most amazing discovery since Tutankhamun. Never mind there's no axe or saw in sight, because right in front of him is a workstation to die for. The collapsible picnic table and fold-up garden chairs were probably dumped here and forgotten when the owners left. Plastic and lightweight aluminium. One of the chairs is missing its seat, but the other looks fine. After two quick trips the table and serviceable chair are in situ in the sitting room, and looking great. A wipe-down with a ragged tea-towel he'd found under the sink and it's goodbye to coal dust and hello to sparkle-and-shine. Beethoven would have given his ear trumpet to have worked at *this* table. The top is a cracked stretch of blue plastic intended to suggest a summer sky. Not quite the serenity of the stars on a clear night that Beethoven once said inspired the slow movement of his second Razumovsky quartet, but getting there.

Time spent upgrading one feature of a room – in this case the furniture and fittings – usually leads to more time spent upgrading everything else. The torn wallpaper and bare floorboards now look well beyond derelict. Beethoven was legendary for living in an upmarket squalor of dirty dishes, empty wine bottles, unwashed laundry, manuscripts everywhere and a pisspot under the piano – but the great composer was so inspired when he worked that he hardly noticed. One glance round the demolition site of a sitting room confirms that even Beethoven would struggle to be inspired here, unless it was to top himself. Morris is desperate to get creating, but he'll give the upgrading half an hour. The hanging strips of wallpaper are ripped off; the broken bricks and lumps of plaster stuffed into a sack and dragged through to his parents' bedroom. He carts away three bagfuls in all, nearly filling up the hole in the floor. The tea-towel rinsed out, he wipes the windowsill clear of spiderwebs, dead flies and creepy-crawlies. Another rinse, and he wipes the window. A third rinse, and he wipes the floor. Thirty minutes on the button, and job done. The sitting room looks like new. Refreshed, certainly. Unlike him.

He drags the length of floorboard through to the bathroom, lays it over the exposed joists, tugs off his clothes and, keeping well clear of the mould, steps into the spray of warm water.

Showered, shaved and dressed again, Composer Morris is now ready to begin work. Almost. Haydn would never have written his eighty-plus string quartets if he had bothered about the cold, and it would have been super cold in the two hundred-bedroom barn that was Esterházy Palace. And so . . . on with his coat, button it up to the chin. Fingerless gloves would be good. A Russian fur hat would be good. So would central heating.

Though not exactly warming up, he will at least lose heat more slowly. Which is progress. He is reaching into his document case for pen and score pad when . . . suddenly . . . inspiration strikes.

He rushes out to the storeroom, grabs the chisel and is back within seconds.

Next, he drags another length of floorboard through from his parents' bedroom to prop up against the edge of the fireplace fender. His left foot keeping it steady, and with the chisel pressed to the open-grain end, he takes a piece of half-brick in his right hand and starts hammering. At every blow, the chisel is driven further into the length of wood, like a wedge. The split gets wider and deeper until, finally, it gives, snapping in two. These thinner lengths of floorboard are then angled against the wall and easily stomped on. The wood will now fit into the grate. A fire is soon blazing up nicely. He sits down at his desk.

*

On Day Two, once you'd grown big enough to reach the keyboard, you often accompanied your mother at her piano. 'Here's thunder!' you'd cry, your palms slapping down at the end of the piano where the keys were loudest and darkest sounding. Yelling 'Sunshine!', you then rushed to what you knew were high-sounding notes at the other end. On Day One, your mother made sure to keep the piano lid closed and locked.

In Middle Earth there were no days and no locks, and almost no furniture. The boarded-up windows meant the ground floor was always in darkness. Preferring to keep the main room candlelit despite the free electricity, Kyle spent most of his time seated cross-legged on the floor, totally stoned. He and Melody shared a private mattress. The other members of the squat – the friendly hobbits usually numbered between ten and a dozen – dossed down in the empty rooms wherever and whenever the mood took them.

During your first wander round the house, you came upon a battered upright that had been abandoned on the upstairs landing. Too eager to waste time looking for a chair, you knelt in front of the keyboard to give it a test run. It was badly out of tune and several of the yellowed keys were stuck, but at least it was a piano. Having played from memory the opening bars of Beethoven's *Moonlight* sonata, you listened as the jangle of notes faded to silence, and felt, for the first time since climbing down from the lorry on the North Circular, that you really were in London.

That evening you spread your sleeping bag out on the floor next to the piano and in the course of the night lost your virginity to a girl who was gone when you woke up. For a few days you thought you were in love.

Your strength recovered and your spirit healed, you and your sweet young blood were reckoned ready to contribute to the Middle Earth finances. Melody made a phone call. It seemed you were in luck and could start earning first thing the following morning.

'There's nothing to it,' she encouraged you over your breakfast soup and roll. 'Easiest job ever. Don't even need to get dressed.' She advised you to keep your eyes fixed on the ceiling or the far wall until you felt relaxed.

An hour later you were in position – but *relaxed*? Having stepped out from behind your screen, you were completely naked, apart from a cock-hugging pouch. There were dozens of people in the room and all staring directly at *you*, staring like you'd never been stared at before. When you actually counted them, there were only ten.

'Remember, it's not *you* they'll be seeing,' Melody had added. 'To them, you are *not* a person.'

Standing on your small platform, you fixed your gaze on a large red gasometer visible out the window and repeated her advice into yourself several times. Like all advice, it was no more than words – and someone else's words at that.

'Morris will be our model for this week,' announced the art school tutor. 'Now then, relax, hands by your sides. Head tilted a shade to the left, please.'

You did your best, keeping your gaze firmly on the gasometer.

'Good . . . a fraction more . . . well done. Now hold that. Let me know if you're too hot or too cold, and we can adjust the heaters.'

Despite the sunlight pouring into the studio through a line of ceiling-to-floor windows, two double-bar electric fires had been placed near you, tilted up to better direct their heat. The room was warm, but you were roasting. It felt like an all-over, top-to-toe naked red blush. Between two of the large windows hung a wall clock. You had to remain in pose, not moving a finger even, for fifty whole minutes at a time. Watching the second hand crawl slowly round the clock face, you felt yourself crawling round with it, and crawling very, very slowly. In front of each student was a tripod topped with a flat piece of wood about a foot square, and on it a lump of plaster that they were moulding onto a small wire frame.

No way could you crawl round and round that clock face another forty-eight times. You shut your eyes. This was a sculpture class, surely the eyes wouldn't matter? It turned out they did.

While keeping your neck, jaw, cheeks and skull totally still, you let your gaze slide away from the clock to drift downwards. You became aware of the students, the tops of their heads at least. Men and *women*.

Another all-over blush, like you were blushing inside.

Someone approached to stand only inches from you.

'Right, Peter.' The tutor's voice, also very close. 'Measure and note down. It's all about proportion.'

You felt a touch on your shoulder and at once turned to see what the student was . . .

'It's okay, Morris. He's just measuring. Head back in position, please.'

In the brief instant you had broken pose you glimpsed an oil slick of long black hair and beard. There was a whiff of garlic. The student, Peter, was holding what looked like a large pair of compasses; one of the points had grazed your shoulder. The other point then pressed on your right elbow. He took various measurements before returning to his plaster of paris maquette. Other students followed. A couple murmured 'Sorry' or 'Excuse me' if they were clumsy and had pressed the compass points too hard against your skin. You ignored them all. The red gasometer. The red gasometer.

Until . . .

The girl's scent took over your five senses all at once. Patchouli oil. You felt your mouth go dry. Before you could stop yourself, you had glanced down and glimpsed a sweep of liquorice-black hair held in an Indian headband. Her heart-stopping nearness. She was so close, so very close. Any closer and . . .

You weren't standing there, you told yourself. You weren't naked. There was no girl.

But there was, and you were.

You dug your fingernails into your palm and, retaining pose as best you could, clenched every muscle in your body, clenched it tight. You had to think of something else. Anything, and fast.

Hitch-hiking . . . Beethoven . . . Middle Earth . . .

For several seconds you stood all-over rigid, jaw clamped shut and holding your breath. If she carried on measuring for much longer you'd have to make a dash for your screen. Dash? You'd be able to pogo-stick.

Having completed her measurements, the girl glanced up. She caught your eye and gave you a friendly nod of thanks, then returned to her place.

Begging in Trafalgar Square . . . The Vietnam War . . . Jimi Hendrix . . .

Gradually your body eased, your breathing returned to normal and out of nowhere you heard a few notes in your head like on Day Two in the cottage. The notes became a short phrase feeling its way to becoming a melody, becoming familiar. Slow, sad and haunting . . . 'Solveig's Song', from Grieg's *Peer Gynt Suite*, a piece your mother often played on the piano when it was safe.

Soon you were no longer fantasising about the girl, no longer in the crowded studio, no longer naked. You were inside the music and the music was inside you. Fully relaxed, you gave yourself to the theme's rise and fall, letting it drift through and . . .

'Morris?' The teacher was standing right in front of you. 'Time for your break. Well done. Back here in ten, please.'

None of the art college models looked like *models*. The job attracted the waifs and strays, the lonely and the lost. Some would have held their pose the whole day had it involved lying flat on their backs, eyes closed, and stoned mindless. Models were usually paid off the books and so, having made some cash, most simply moved on. Only two had turned it into a career. In her forties and scrawny as a plucked chicken – 'They like my bone structure' – Donna had lived a double life for twenty years.

'When the Diploma Show goes up in summer I'm always terrified my husband will want to come in and see it. He'd go mental.' She grinned. 'Thinks I work in an office.'

A model for over thirty years, Mr Bamber was an institution. He had no first name. Balding and with rolling slabs of fat, he smelled of talcum powder and raw loneliness.

This was your first real glimpse into the adult world. Until then, you had never been close-up on a daily basis to any adults except your parents, who didn't count, nor did your teachers. Donna gossiped on the bench and asked about your family. You told her about your father being a salesman who was often away from home, and about your mother keeping hens and teaching you the piano. When she asked if you missed them, you made her laugh by telling her that what you didn't miss was the haggis your mother cooked every Saturday, then listing what went into it. Donna often chatted about her three kids and it was like she was lifting the roof off a happily chaotic doll's house. One day, however, you happened to glance up as she was approaching the model's bench and were shocked to see the stricken look on her face. It vanished the instant she saw you. She smiled, sat down and was as cheerful and gossipy as ever. Mr Bamber always sat on the same spot, staring straight in front of him. When his name was called, he would give no response, but rise unhurriedly to his feet and, in its own good time, his stately bulk would follow the tutor down the corridor to disappear from sight. After several attempts to make conversation with him, you gave up.

'Fancy coming to a party?' one of the girls had called to you over the top of your screen. It was the end of the first week and you were getting into your clothes before heading back to Middle Earth. 'I'll leave the address on the stool out here.'

'Thanks,' you called back. 'Sounds great!'

There was no reply; the girl had already left.

Several parties and several weekends later, your

Friday and Saturday nights became an end-of-the-week blur. So, too, did the drinks and the girls. Drink made you feel good, more drink made you feel better. Day One and Day Two seemed no more than a bad dream you had woken from and your life would now roll on effortlessly from day to day, party to party, girl to girl, drink to drink, and would surely never stop.

It was a week before Christmas, the last hour of the last pose of the year, and you could sense the students' pre-holiday excitement. Red-berried bunches of holly hung from the studio doorway and lay along the windowsills, tinsel trailing from some of the tripods. Mistletoe dangled from one of the lights, and someone had draped your screen with red and green streamers. There was excited chit-chat about going home; travel arrangements were discussed, small presents exchanged. Going home for Christmas had never even occurred to you and, by the time you emerged from behind your screen, the studio was deserted. You pulled on your rucksack stuffed with towel, trunks and clean clothes for a pre-Yuletide swim. As you made your way along the empty corridors to the exit, your footsteps echoed back, sounding very solitary. Outside, it was snowing.

No more pouch, no more parties, no more cash. You had nine pounds, seventeen shillings and tuppence to last until the new term started in January. Your contribution to Middle Earth would cut into that. Would there be a Christmas buzz at the squat? You pictured Kyle wearing a Santa hat and rolling Christmas-cracker-sized joints decorated with robins and snowflakes, hobbits wearing party hats and everyone singing while you picked out carols on the yellowed keys.

The snow was soon falling thicker. Forget the swimming pool. You sped through the streets, eager to get to your hot soup, chunk of bread and the half-bottle for afters that you'd bought yourself as a pre-Christmas treat. Only a few more houses to go and . . .

Had you taken a wrong turning? Wrong street, wrong house? Slithering the last few yards of snow up to the gate. Right street, right house, but . . .

The Middle Earth front door was boarded up, the garden littered with clothes, shoes, someone's kaftan, smashed crockery, wall hangings; Melody's soup pot lay on its side and chopped vegetables spilled out in a frozen tide . . . everything getting covered in snow. Everything getting soaked, ruined. Your sleeping bag sprawled sodden in an ice puddle; the piano was on its back, helpless, its insides choked with drifting snow.

A handwritten notice was pinned to the door, the ink already smeared but still legible: KEEP OUT. ANYTHING NOT REMOVED WILL BE BINNED.

The snow was coming down heavier by the minute, settling on your hair, gusting icily into your face. Staring at the remains of life in Middle Earth strewn across the cement, you felt chilled to the bone and yet, at the same time, you felt nothing.

What was left to feel?

*

Sitting at his sky-blue desk, coat buttoned up to his chin and sleeping bag laid across his knees, Morris pulls his score pad into position and picks up his pen.

McGibbon had said he wanted a tune, ten minutes max. Unfortunately, Morris doesn't *do* tunes. To create slot-machine jingles, he plays about on his desktop, coming up with the electronic gurgles and whooshes that will be triggered whenever someone wins or loses. His remit is simple: get the punters to put more coins in the slot. He can read music, but can he write it? He knows he wants to, with all his heart and soul. *No squeaky gate* means no atonal stuff that's all over the place, like Boulez, say, or Xenakis. After seventy years' silence he's ready and more to sing out a good tune, a *cri de coeur* that's been building up inside him his whole life. He can *feel* it. All he needs are the right notes. But ten minutes is very long for a tune, longer than some of Mozart's early symphonies. Pop tunes don't last half that, so he'll think of it as three tunes strung together: a three-movement quartet, Fast – slow – fast, like a Vivaldi concerto. It worked for il Prete Rosso – the man wrote more than five hundred of them.

Nothing fancy. Divide the melody between the first and second violin, the bass line between viola and cello. Add a short cadenza for solo violin to the first movement and he can call it a chamber concerto for string quartet. Give it a snappy title and he's good to go. There will be no payment, but does that really matter? He can live on his pension and still churn out the odd jingle, if needs must. The important thing is to write music that feels true, music that is *his*. If Beethoven had been offered a million ducats on condition that he stopped writing music, the great composer would have refused. It would have meant stopping being himself. Morris stopped being himself many years ago. Since then, he's drunk enough wine and cognac to lay down the burden his life has become, drunk it on a daily basis. But not any more. Starting today, it's going to be music all the way, *his* music, and before it is too late. Here, in the house where he was born, and for the first time in his life, he will become the true Morris Magellan.

Key signature? He'll trust his imagination and wait to see what emerges. The quartet will reveal itself in its own good time. As a mere amanuensis to his creativity, his job is to sit calmly, clear his mind, focus and be ready to receive. This is not the same as making up slot-machine jingles, nothing like it – this will be the real thing.

Two hours, three lengths of floorboard and four botched sheets ripped from the score pad later, he has his snappy title. At the head of sheet number five he prints in block capitals: *NO ORCHESTRA NEEDED, Opus 1.* What he needs now is inspiration.

After a lifetime spent hemmed in on all sides by crowded city streets, traffic and pedestrians, tenements and supermarkets, endless noise, bustle and vexation, it is time to stride out into the glorious freedom of the countryside. Like Beethoven, what he needs are open spaces, the sky above him and the distant horizon drawing him ever forward. Following in the great man's footsteps, he will listen to the wind in the trees, to the rushing of the streams, to birdsong and lowing cattle. He will go wherever the mood takes him, singing out his melodies loud and strong like Beethoven did; he will raise his arms and conduct the clouds. If he meets anyone, he will call out hello, and keep moving. If anyone waves to him, he will wave back, and keep moving.

Pulling the garden gate behind him, the new Morris steps out into a new world. Who needs Courvoisier when he has a whole planet to stand on, a planet rolling forever through the vastness of space and willing to take him along for the ride? Mahler's *Das Lied von der Erde* – turbo-charged! The rush of solar winds, the pull of unearthly gravities will surely inspire—

A see-through shutter slams down. Right in front of him. Sudden. Abrupt.

The planet stops turning.

There are cars parked everywhere and people coming and going in the street. There are prams, buggies, dogs. The rookery beyond the village hall bursts into an uproar of *kaah, kaah*. Kids are hullaballooing, chasing each other, laughing and yelling . . .

While he . . .

While he remains trapped on the wrong side of the shutter, pinned by the force of the stalled planet whose gravity pushes upwards through the soles of his feet, gripping him tight. He can hardly breathe, never mind move.

Tied to the railings outside the village hall is a sign announcing:

END OF WINTER SALE OF WORK
To be opened by Mrs Cairns
EVERYONE WELCOME
SATURDAY 14 MARCH 10 till 3
ENTRY £1
(Lucky ticket raffle at 12 noon)

'There's aye a guid turn-oot fer the sale.' An elderly man has come up beside him. Cap, white beard and smiling like the village Santa.

'Looks busy all right,' Morris manages to call out from behind his shutter, doing his best to sound pleased. Which he suddenly discovers he is. Forget Beethoven's solitary woods and fields – so nineteenth century, so kailyard! The buzz and bustle of twenty-first-century Scottish men and women shall be his inspiration!

The shutter has dissolved into fresh air and sunlight, and once again he feels the planet's comforting rush under his feet, carrying him ever-forward.

'They'll hae scones an cakes an tea,' says Santa. 'An ye dinna want tae miss the raffle. Yer first time here, is it?'

'I . . .'

'A tidy wee place thon.' Santa points back at Morris's cottage. 'Or wis. Peety it's bin empty sae lang. A wunner it's still staundin.'

Has Santa taken his 'I' for a Scots *aye* of agreement?

'No, I was meaning that I – I *have* been here before. Quite a while back.'

'Oh, aye?'

He feels he has been caught out in a lie.

'I'm Jimmy, Jimmy Blakely. Been here aa ma life,' continues the old man as the two of them approach the hall.

'Pleased to meet you, Jimmy.' They shake hands. 'I'm Morris.'

'Morris, eh?' Jimmy uses a stick to help him up the steps.

Does the old man recognise him? He is about to explain when Jimmy stumbles. Morris takes his arm to help steady him.

'Maist fowk caa me Jimmy the Post. Back then I delivered aabody's letters in the village. Ma bike at the stairt, then ma van.'

Jimmy the Post had lived with his parents in the cottage directly opposite. Probably still does. Morris wants to say he remembers him, but the words won't come out, like they're filling up his mouth, like they need to get themselves sorted before they can tell the truth.

'A haill pun tae git in. Mak sair ye git yer money's warth!' Jimmy laughs and disappears into the crowded hall.

The place is packed, filled with the din of voices. Too many people, too many chances to be found out. Which doesn't make any sense. So what is he worrying about? He has nothing to hide.

The place is packed, and here's him with his coat still buttoned. He's sweating already. The noise, the crush. What the hell's he doing at a Sale of Work? He is supposed to be in his cottage, writing his string quartet. At the very least, he's supposed to be wandering the countryside like Beethoven, seeking inspiration. He tries heading back to the door, but the press of people coming in pushes him towards a line of stalls. Soon he is so close to one of the tables its sharp edge digs into his thigh. The stallholder looks at him and smiles. 'Can I help—?'

Don't ask me anything, he wants to say. He wants to get away, far away, and for one crazy moment imagines leaping onto the table as it rises up into the air to sweep a circle round the rafters before soaring out the front door, carrying him and the homemade bread and cakes up, up and into the clouds like he was on a magic carpet.

The woman is still looking at him.

Once he starts buying he can't seem to stop. Homemade gingerbread and scones. Onto the next stall – honey, eggs. Another stall – cheese, a fruit cordial. Another stall – another cordial, some jam. More stalls. Homemade butter, more cheese, more honey, cramming it all into a supermarket bag he has been given. Is he taking on ballast to help keep himself upright? He zigzags from stall to stall like he's careering downhill, round hairpin bends, and the brakes have failed. When the plastic handle rips, another stallholder gives him a sturdier bag so oversized he has to hold it out in front.

And he's off again – hurtling from stall to stall as if still trying to side-step that terrible crash he could never avoid in the end. So desperate he was, grabbing a girlfriend, a job, a car, a marriage, a mortgage, promotion, children. Holding onto them for dear life, like now.

He has reached a plant stall, a trestle table that's a tangle of jungle-green stalks, leaves and creepers – thin green, thick green, spiky green, swollen bulbous green. A rainforest. He half-expects to hear parrots and the chatter of chimps, and to see snakes coiling everywhere – only to find he is looking at the red puffer who has colonised his parents' garden. The man, mid-thirties at most, is wearing a T-shirt that says: BLAME ME, I VOTED BREXIT.

Morris's arms are beginning to ache; he has bought far too much already. He starts to back away . . . and collides with an elderly woman. He apologises.

'Nae hairm done. Fair thrang, eh?' she shouts above the din as she moves off.

'Certainly is,' he shouts back.

'Hi there.' The ex-Brexiteer bellows out from behind his rainforest. Morris pretends not to hear, but the crowd is too dense to let him make for the door. Also, bumping into the woman has made his ballast slide to one side. He gives the bag a shake to resettle it, glances up and manages to look surprised.

'Oh, I didn't see it was you!' he hears himself call back, and immediately wishes he hadn't. Another lie.

'I seen ye oot on yer doorstep this mornin. Didnae ken the place wis sold?' comes the friendly prompt.

Someone pushes him forward again, forcing him hard up against the plant stall.

'Ye'll hae fetched up gey late last nicht?'

'What?' Morris has to yell to be heard.

'Said ye must've fetched up late last nicht?'

'Bad snow above Moffat.' He turns to leave. Meaning it as an exit line, he adds, 'Like coming over the Russian Steppes.'

'Whit's that? Steps? You walked?'

'No, I mean . . .'

Standing beside puffer man is a small woman, slim, dark, delicate and a few years younger, a woman from the other side of the world. Mrs Puffer?

'I'm Mervin. Call me Merv.' The man holds out his hand through the rainforest.

Clutching the massive bag to his chest, he shakes hands. 'Morris.'

'Stockin up in case o a lockdoon, ir ye?'

'Pardon?'

But Merv has turned to the woman. 'This here's Morris frae the auld cottage, like ah telt ye. Morris, ma wife, Rosanna.'

'Pleased to meet you.' An American accent. As she has shorter arms, Morris is forced to extend his hand further into the rainforest this time, and to lean forward.

'Mind the—' yells Merv.

Having no more than grazed Rosanna's fingertips with his own, Morris snatches back his hand.

Music is the human spirit expressed as sound moving through time, and is a genuine miracle. The same theme can be restated, elaborated and developed – different keys, different harmonies, different tempi – until an initial melodic gesture achieves its deepest and most satisfying expression. Unlike everyday life where everything happens only once, and forever, and where a clumsy gesture will remain so, for all time.

'Sorry,' Morris cries out, jerking a corner of the bag clear of a haze of greenery, a spray of plant fronds fine as mist. 'Sorry.' The plant wobbles briefly. Then steadies. A close thing, but no damage done.

But as he swings round to remove himself and his purchases from any risk of causing harm, Morris's sleeve catches at the supporting stick of a purple-and-white orchid.

Instantly, the scene at the plant stall splits into two separate time zones:

1. Merv and Rosanna stand motionless, seemingly overwhelmed. On their side of the rainforest, time has stopped. Their faces, illumined as if from within, appear freeze-framed. In horror. And fury.

2. On Morris's side of the rainforest, time has sped up. Alarm. Panic. Trapped in a terrifying chain of cause-and-effect where possibilities become probabilities become certainties in an accelerating series that can only end badly, he clutches the over-sized bag in an effort to keep it clear of further disaster. Tugging his sleeve this way and that, he wrenches the orchid's supporting stick from side to side. His wrist flattens a white bloom, then crushes a purple one. Unable to bring a completely free hand into play, he keeps on tugging. The plant sways, wobbles. Petals like so many brushstrokes of pure colour are sent cascading to the floor. To be followed a moment later by the plant itself. And the plant next to

it. He steps back too abruptly, knocking plant number three off the table.

Coming in quick succession, the three loud crashes are followed by an even louder silence. Morris glances down. He takes in the carnage of broken stems, petals, earth, bamboo supports and smashed pottery. The silence is charged with tension. With threat.

'Tak'd me three year tae grow them!' Having broken out of its freeze-frame, Merv's anger booms across the hall and comes echoing back from every side.

Morris can manage only the faintest, most faraway-sounding 'I'm so sorry, so sorry, so sorry . . .' Wishing he too was faraway.

The hall recovers its confident hustle-bustle almost at once.

And he's back at the plant stall. Back facing explosive-red Merv, closed-faced Rosanna. Back to where half a rainforest lies destroyed on the floor.

He offers to pay.

'It's no the money.'

He offers to clear up the mess.

'Leave it. Ye've done enough.'

He turns to Rosanna. Her eyes, mouth, cheeks, lips are hard and rigid.

He places his oversized bag on the floor.

Before Merv can manage another put-down, Morris has pulled out his wallet and placed a twenty-pound note on the table. 'It was an accident, Mervin. I apologise.' His voice is firm.

No response.

How much *are* orchids? Three years has been mentioned. Care and attention has been mentioned. He adds another twenty.

Merv takes the notes in a scrunched handful. To throw them back in Morris's face?

This is surely his moment to leave. He bends down to begin scooping the spilled earth into an empty Tesco bag he's noticed under the table. One of the pots is only cracked and its orchid more or less undamaged. He lifts it up carefully, then lowers it into the bag. A white bloom remains sticking out of the top like a flag of distress.

Morris cringes as he hears himself attempt a joke. 'Might as well get something for my money.'

No response.

Having scooped up most of the earth together with what's left of the other orchids, he gets to his feet.

'They'll never survive.' Merv's parting words are clearly meant to push him back down onto his knees.

He is shocked to hear a burst of applause all around him and feels a rush of cold sweat. Has the whole hall been watching his clumsy—?

But it is not him they are clapping. Instead, the crowd has turned to face a small stage at the front where a woman who looks pure county with her silk scarf, twinset and pearls is making an announcement.

Someone pokes him in the arm.

'Yer the wunner, Morris!' It's Jimmy.

'What?'

'The special prize draw. Mine's echty-three.' The old man holds up a green cloakroom ticket. 'They gied ye the yin efter me. Yers maun be echty-fower.'

Bewildered, Morris stands holding his plastic bag of earth and orchids . . . *maun be echty-fower* . . . He understands the Scots, but the words make no sense. Jimmy expects him to do something?

'Yer the wunner, Morris!'

'Green eighty-four,' calls out the woman.

'Oot wi yer ticket, man!'

Jimmy looks so pleased for him that Morris starts fumbling in his jeans. He pulls out a handful of pocket stuff – supermarket receipts, keys, a used paper hanky. A scrunch of green.

'Here he is!' Jimmy gives him a gentle shove towards the stage.

There's another burst of applause. Everyone has turned to look at him. A path clears.

'Ah, a new face in the village.' A few years younger than he is, ash blonde and her hair being left to grey naturally, the woman has a friendly smile. The remains of a private school accent are wrapped round a warm Borders brogue.

As he approaches the front of the hall, Morris catches sight of what must be the special prize standing on a small table, wrapped in red tissue paper. Instantly, the hall and everyone else in it vanishes. Only he and his prize remain. That, and the shock of it.

On automatic, he manages to return the woman's smile, to tell her his name and where he is from. What

45

has brought him to the village? she asks. The words *here for the fishing* come out of his mouth by themselves, and he hopes their blandness will bring the conversation to an end.

But it doesn't. The sharpness of tone in the woman's next remark is accusatory almost. It pins him firmly to the present moment, in the crowded hall, the focus of everyone's attention. She is looking directly at him, waiting for him to reply. *Everyone* is waiting for him to reply. But all he can think of is his prize, his fucking prize. Tell them *Thanks but no thanks*? Which would be insulting the whole village, all in one go. But, fuck, he doesn't want it. Fuck, fuck . . . Pretend to fumble, then drop it when it's handed over? He'll get the sympathy vote at least. Won't he? Maybe. But maybe he'll fumble the fumble. Fuck, fuck . . .

His mind seizes up; he's unable to take in what the woman has actually said. Some of her words . . . *too many visitors who . . . the Annan's nearly fished out . . .* have got through to him. Not only has he been cast in the role of an outsider taking away a prize that should have stayed in the village, but he's clearly been judged as someone set on depleting what little remains of the local fishing stock.

'I . . .' It's on the tip of his tongue to reassure them he is no stranger, he was born in the village and used to fish the Annan as a boy, very likely with some of the people here in the hall today. He wants to tell them the truth, but once again the words pile up in his mouth. He wants to tell them to keep their prize, but instead hears his voice coming to the rescue with a joke. 'With my kind of luck, the fish will be safe enough!'

Which gets a few laughs. Not many.

The woman and her pearls haven't finished. Her friendly smile back in place, she concludes the presentation with practised ceremony.

'Congratulations, Morris, and we wish you a very pleasant stay here in our village.'

He accepts the prize with care, with caution, as if, despite its festive wrapping, he has been entrusted with an unexploded bomb.

He says thank you. There is a smattering of applause. Polite.

The glass shutter slams back down. Morris, his bag of orchids and the unexploded bomb on one side, the hall and everyone else in it on the other. He edges away from the small stage and heads for the door. The crowd parts in front of him. He starts to speed up. Forget dropping it, he's just had a better idea. Much better.

Outside, he pauses. Things could not have gone worse. And so—

Straight home, and do it. Straight home, and do it.

Clutching his bag of orchids and the unexploded bomb, he hurries down the steps, onto the road, past the parked cars. No looking left, no looking right. Ramrod stiff every step of the way.

Do it! Do it!

Pushing open the gate, hurrying up the path, key in the door. Orchid bag dumped on the floor.

Do it! Do it!

Crossing to the sink, tearing off the tissue paper. Whisky. The Famous Grouse.

Do it! Do it!

But he doesn't. Not immediately.

Which means he doesn't.

He hesitates. Which means he still doesn't.

He takes a deep breath, anticipating the aroma of . . .

Do it! Do it!

. . . Picturing the sunlit-brown liquid he is about to send swirling and whirlpooling round the sink before it disappears down the . . .

He can almost taste the . . .

DO IT!

He breaks the seal and—

There's a knock at the door.

He freezes. Caught in the act.

Slowly . . . slowly . . .

Slowly, so as not to make a sound and still holding the bottle tight in his hand, he turns away from the sink.

They might go away.

Another knock. A red face appears at the window, staring straight in.

Merv. For fuck's sake. Not now.

'Morris! I ken yer in there.'

Without thinking, Morris whips the bottle behind his back and goes to the door.

'Wantin tae apologise. Ah wis oot o order back there.' Merv holds out his hand. 'Ah'm really sorry. Git cairrit awaa sometimes. Tak ma flooers owre serious.'

Keeping the bottle well out of sight, Morris shakes hands. 'I'm sorry about your flowers.'

'Fowks' nebs wur fair pit oot o joint, some o them, yer winnin the whisky like thon.' He peers past Morris into the kitchen. 'Here for the fishin ye said, but ah heard ye've bocht the place.'

'Well, I'm . . .'

'Seein yer doun tae the flairboards, nou's yer chance tae git in the central heatin.' He shakes his head. 'Means a carryvan in the gairden.'

'What's left of it.' The comeback is out before he can stop it.

'Whit?' Genuine puzzlement. Merv's arrival must post-date the land grab.

'I'm only staying for—'

'Yin thing,' Merv interrupts. 'Ah cannae mind if Davie Robson hid his lum swept oot or no afore flittin, said it wis fair needit. Widnae want yer hoose burnin doun oan yer first day.' He starts to edge away from the doorway. 'Need tae git back tae ma stall.' He points to the ground. 'An ah brocht ye yer stuff.'

Morris notices the oversized bag on the doorstep. 'Thank you, Merv. Very kind of you to . . .'

Merv is fumbling in his pocket. 'Here's a tenner back – ye gied me owre much – an here's ma caird, fer the central heatin.' He hurries off.

'Really kind of you, thanks!' Morris shouts after and brings the large supermarket bag inside. He stashes the two cheeses, the butter, gingerbread and scones in the mouse-proof bucket and lines up the jars of honey and jam, the eggs and the rest of his expanded food store on the draining board. Feeling calmer, he stands the whisky bottle on the sitting-room mantelpiece. He will show it who is boss, and ignore it. Placed on the windowsill, the surviving orchid makes the place look a little brighter already.

He props Merv's card up on the mantelpiece: *Merv Wilson the central heating specialist: Let Merv keep you and your family warm all winter.* There is a mobile number.

A busy start to his day, but still no real work done. His best plan will be to decide it is lunchtime. Thanks to his visit to the hall, he is spoilt for choice and settles on some bread, cheese and pickled onions, and, for afters, a banana and a slice of gingerbread, the honey spooned on thick. His feast laid out on the sky table, he gets out his iPod and dines, as the Archbishop of Salzburg often did, to an early Mozart serenade. Everything washed down with a mug of elderflower cordial, murky looking but delicious, followed by a mug of tea.

Work? He'll need to chisel another floorboard. Merv mentioned the chimney maybe catching fire, maybe needing swept . . .

All at once he feels really, really, really tired. And no wonder. Since getting the commission he has hardly had a moment to sit down and relax. It's been non-stop rush-rush-rush: sorting out his flat before leaving, driving for hours in the dark, too late to bed, too little sleep, cleaning up the sitting room, breaking into the storeroom, setting up his workstation, making a start on his quartet, then the fiasco at the village hall. No wonder he is exhausted. Siesta time. He unzips his sleeping bag, opening it out like a quilt. The instant his head hits the holdall he is out for the count.

★

No more Middle Earth, no more big city and one further basic truth learned: bad weather means bad lifts, or none at all, especially in midwinter, especially at night. Car drivers don't want their smart interiors to get wet; lorry drivers concentrating to stay on the road don't always see you.

Getting clear of London took hours and from then on the lifts were few and far between. By the time a slow-moving furniture van dropped you off at a petrol station somewhere up the A1 it was well past midnight and you were exhausted. The pump man on duty took pity and let you bed down on the floor in the back office, next to a Christmas tree.

The morning started cold and sunny and the lifts picked up. The further north you got the more wintry it felt. When rain turned to hail at Scotch Corner you headed into a transport café. Warm, dry and brightly lit, with a welcoming smell of grease and chips. A tea urn steamed on the counter. A jukebox decked in tinsel was belting out Nancy Sinatra's 'These Boots Were Made for Walking', while some of the drivers at the formica tables stamped out the chorus. Paper streamers hung from the rafters of the corrugated-iron roof.

Having put yourself outside a plate of sausage, egg and chips, you went back to the till to ask for some small change. The telephone box was outside. The hail had stopped. Would it be Day One or Day Two? At worst, you could always hang up. You put in enough coins, heard them tinkle, then dialled, ready to press Button B if your father answered. You tried five times and got number unobtainable. You dialled for the operator.

'Sorry, caller, this number has been disconnected.'

'But it can't be. Can you try again? Please.'

The woman did. Still disconnected. 'Are you sure it is the correct—?'

'But . . . it's my parents.'

There was a pause. 'I'm really sorry, caller.'

Back to your seat in the café. A card from your mother only a fortnight before had said nothing about them moving. She would have told you. Surely. You pictured the heavy black phone sitting on its spot on the kitchen windowsill. It was an old phone, lots of crossed lines, bad connections . . . Halfway into the 'Can't Buy Me Love' chorus, you let your head rest on the formica.

'Come on, Sleeping Beauty!' Not an angry voice. Someone was shaking your shoulder. Not hard, but not giving up either. 'It's time you were . . .'

You opened your eyes. It was the counter man.

'. . . hitting the trail. I'm expecting a load of regulars in soon and need the space.'

You glanced over at the steamed-up window, at the darkness outside.

'Sorry.' You started getting to your feet.

'No rush. I've brought you another tea. Set you up for the road. On the house.' The man's kindness nearly made you burst into tears.

Your tea finished, you carried your mug across to the till. 'Thank you. That was really great.'

The counter man glanced up. 'Are you coming or going? From home, I mean?'

'I suppose I'm . . .'

Just then the door opened and a blast of cold air blew in half a dozen drivers.

'Here comes trouble!' the owner called over.

You managed a smile, picked up your rucksack and left. You took up position at the exit. Carry on north, or cross the road and head back to London? You had no idea. Leave it to fate?

A cattle truck was approaching. You stuck out your thumb. With a hiss of air brakes the lorry came to a stop. The driver shouted down that he was making for Penrith.

'Great, thanks!' you shouted back, and climbed in.

It was well past seven p.m. when a car-transporter out of Carlisle took you across the border into Scotland. On his way to the Stranraer ferry the driver dropped you at Lochmaben, which meant a three-mile slog in the dark with little chance of a lift. At least the rain had stopped. Wind whined in the telegraph wires lining the road; it tugged at the trees and hedgerows as if wanting to tear them out by the roots, and sent clouds racing across the moon. You hunched your shoulders, pushing your way forward.

An hour later you reached the turn-off to the village and the slog became uphill. Having tried to phone again at Lochmaben, and with the same result, you still kept trying to convince yourself your parents hadn't moved. Your mum would have told you, definitely. Definitely. You allowed yourself to picture a coal-and-log fire blazing in the sitting room. Your mother looks up from her knitting as you walk in the door. She is so very pleased to see you, so very—

The wind was at its fiercest at the brow of the hill, but here, at least, it was at your back. Gust after gust thrust you down the steep descent into the village. Past the church, the farm, the schoolteacher's house where a light still burned. Worn out though you were, the wind was blowing so hard that by the time you could make out the cottage, its Snowcemmed brickwork a ghostly white in the moonlight, you were almost running down the hill towards it. Only the weight of your rucksack kept you from being lifted off your feet.

Knowing the gate would screech, you climbed over the garden wall and made your way as soundlessly as you could round to the front of the house. The sitting room curtains were pulled and the light was on. Someone, at least, was in. Fingers crossed it was your mother, and she was alone. You had a quick look through the gap in the garage door, hoping you wouldn't see your father's car, but it was too dark to see anything. So he might be at home, or he might not. Was it Day One, or Day Two?

If your parents had moved, it would be no day at all.

House doors were locked only at bedtime, and often not even then. You stepped quietly into the dark kitchen, into a warm smell of frying. Onions, liver. It felt good to be out of the wind and you stood for a few moments, catching your breath. In the faint light you noticed the phone was no longer on the windowsill. Had it really been—?

Just then you heard your father's voice coming through from the sitting room. Which was bad enough; worse was the tone he spoke in: so much calmer and more normal sounding than you could believe possible. Never once had he addressed you like that. He was saying something about getting a guinea fowl for their Christmas from the Marchmont estate. Your mother's response was all but inaudible. Several times you were on the point of throwing open the door to walk in and surprise them. Only to hesitate at the last moment.

You imagined the shock your father would have at seeing you: he breaks off in mid-phrase, glares at you in sudden fury. He is on his feet, advancing towards you, shouting. So vivid did this feel that you were surprised to find yourself still in the kitchen, listening to the murmur of their conversation.

Instead, you went into the small room off the kitchen. You didn't dare put on the light. Were you afraid he might hear the click of the switch and come through to find you? By moonlight you could see it was no longer your bedroom. No bed, no bedside cabinet, no bookcase, no wardrobe. The set of golf clubs in the corner, the fishing rods, the pair of waders, the armchair, the strong cigarette smell, the heavy outdoor jackets and waterproofs hanging on hooks along the wall: your bedroom had become your father's private den.

Unfastening the curtains from their rail, you wrapped them around you, lay down on the floor and were asleep within minutes.

Most likely, your mother would have brought any late-night tea things through to wash in the sink and leave on the draining board to dry. She would have turned off the kitchen light and gone to bed without giving your old room a second glance.

You were woken by first light coming in the uncurtained window. From the kitchen cupboard you liberated a packet of digestives and a tin of corned beef. As you went out the door, you snatched up a pint of milk from the step. Passing the sitting room, you saw a light come on.

Halfway up the steep brae out of the village, you heard the screech of the gate and glanced back to see a figure hurrying out onto the road. Your mother? Your father? You couldn't be certain and strained to see. If it was your mother you would sprint back down the hill, throw your arms around her and—

A second figure appeared. Your father. He stood and shook his fist at you. At the top of the hill you stopped again, and were in time to see him leading your mother back towards the house. You continued past the farm where a collie came dashing out to bark at you. You kept going. Behind you, another day was beginning for your parents and everyone in the village. When you reached the large Scots pine beyond the church you found a tuft of grass dry enough to sit on. Leaning back against the trunk, you drank the milk and breakfasted on the corned beef and biscuits.

*

Morris is woken by the *slam-slam-slam* of a door. Wind is howling down the chimney; wind is rattling the window in its frame. It's light outside and he must have been so tired he's gone and slept right round the clock. Shows how right he was to come here.

Slam-slam-slam. Probably the storeroom door he forced open and left unfastened. The whisky bottle is still on the mantelpiece, and still untouched. A real achievement. Not a drop for two whole days and two whole nights. Which makes him feel good, recharged and raring to get to work on the quartet. From now on he will get up early every morning and work; he will go for inspirational strolls through the countryside, then return to the cottage and work. He will work and, when needed, he will relax. Sometimes life can really be that simple.

Having slept in his clothes means he can hit the new day running. Ditto if he bypasses the shower. All that getting wet and getting dried will only slow him down and—

Stop right there. That's dosser talk, not real-composer-who-is-writing-real-music-for-real-musicians talk.

After a proper shower and a proper shave Morris steps outside to greet the new day. Threatening clouds and a darkening sky that's getting darker by the minute. A real storm looks on the way. He'll skip the inspirational walk – no sense in drenching himself twice over! Some Coco Pops and two slices of bread and honey later, he returns to the sitting room. Time to chisel a floorboard and light the fire.

But suppose Merv is right and the chimney really does need swept? With one hand on the mantelpiece to steady himself, he peers up into the sooty blackness. Out of nowhere he feels a *frisson* of unexpected excitement. As a little boy he had sensed that when calling up to Santa Claus he was entering a realm forever closed to his father. And here he is now, once again standing in the fireplace. He should make a wish!

Inspiration for his quartet. He almost says the words out loud but, instead, laughs to himself: 'A warm room to work in and some lightbulbs to see by. And a mug with a handle!'

He lifts the picnic table and chair over to the window for better light, then, coat buttoned up and sleeping bag over his knees, he takes his seat at his workstation. Candle and matches placed close-by, just in case. And if neighbour Merv pops up at the window to ask what he's doing? *Writing a string quartet!* he'll call back. A conversation stopper, with bells on. Ting-a-ling! Having taken a sip of the black tea and added a carton of milk to the Santa wish list, he glances over at the Grouse perched on the mantelpiece. Time was when cognac helped him get his mornings started, helped him float his boat and take his bearings on the day ahead. Not any more. When a sip is too much, the whole bottle is never enough, and this morning he's not even going to be tempted because . . .

Because what he will do is . . .

No hesitation, no second thoughts, and even better than pouring seventy centilitres' worth of Famous Grouse down the sink . . .

Don't think it, do it!

Next moment he has thrown off the sleeping bag, jumped up from his picnic chair and grabbed the bottle from the mantelpiece. Next-next moment he is marching out the house, down the path, out the gate and along the road. It's still early and nobody's about, thank goodness. A lightning dart up the front steps and back down again. Mission accomplished. The bottle of whisky now stands outside the door of the village hall as if delivered with the morning milk. He grins to himself, imagining the look on the finder's face. Their surprise and delight. Well, they are welcome to it. All those noses out of joint, like Merv said. They will appreciate his sensitivity and—

The hall door opens; someone is coming out.

'Don't move!' he calls up.

It is the woman with the pearls. She looks down at him. 'Pardon?'

'The bottle. Mind you don't—'

'What on earth?' She picks up the whisky. 'This was first prize in the raffle.' She pauses, looks at him closely.

'You won it, didn't you? Don't you want it?'

'Well . . .' Morris begins.

'Prefer a single malt, would you?'

'No. No. Not that at all.' He takes a step back. 'Fact is, I don't drink. I was hoping that someone else might . . .'

'So you put it on the *doorstep*?' She is clearly bewildered.

'Would *you* like it?'

She laughs. 'Very kind of you, I'm sure. I'm sorry, I don't remember your name.' She holds the bottle out to him.

And with that, the unexploded bomb is back in his hands.

'Morris. Morris Magellan,' he manages to reply.

'Ah, yes. Here for the fishing you said.' Is she checking up on his story? Doesn't she believe him? In a more serious tone, she adds, 'I apologise for that dig about the Annan being nearly fished out by visitors. I'm strong on green issues and tend to go charging in both feet first. It was rude of me, and quite unnecessary.'

'Like I said, the fish are safe enough with me around!'

He needs to get back. Soon as he can. Pour the whisky straight down the sink. All of it.

'I'm Jess, by the way.' A firm handshake. They start to walk slowly in the direction of his cottage. 'You know you are the talk of the village?'

'Me? I've hardly seen anyone, hardly talked to anyone.' He'll need to hold his nose while emptying out the bottle – he can't risk getting tempted by the aroma.

'No need,' she laughs. 'The village probably knows more about you than you do!'

He grins. 'That wouldn't be hard. There's not much to . . .' On second thoughts, better to upend the bottle, leave it leaning against the side of the sink to *glug* itself out.

'Merv says you sleep on the floor.'

'Sort of. It's a bit like camping, at the moment.'

'Jimmy the Post says he remembers your mother . . .' She pauses. '. . . And your father.'

'Jimmy's right. I was born here.' It feels a relief to tell someone the truth at last. Jess seems a nice woman. Attractive. Bright eyes. 'I'm here to work, actually . . . as well as for the fishing,' he adds quickly. 'Work mostly, though.'

'You're a builder?'

'What? No, no. I'm . . . I'm a composer.' Which feels like a lie, but it's not.

Jess has come to a standstill next to a parked car, a white Golf. 'That's a real surprise! You're famous?'

Time for some back-pedalling. 'I got into it by accident. I used to be a business executive. Majestic Biscuits?'

'They're famous!'

'More famous than me, that's for sure! Then one day I thought: did I want to spend the rest of my life administering biscuits? So I left.'

'That was brave.'

It is like he is laying her a trail of breadcrumbs to

follow, and he wants to stop. But he can't. 'Not really. First sensible thing I ever did.' He is telling her the truth, but it keeps coming out sideways.

'What about your family? What did they . . .?'

'To be honest, I wasn't the easiest person to live with. The work was very high stress.'

'Wasn't your wife glad when you packed it in?'

'Too late by then.' More breadcrumbs, too many. 'Anyway, it turned out best for everyone. Mary has her new life and I have mine. In fact, that's why I am here!' Back on solid ground again. 'I am working on a commission for a string quartet, and when I saw the advert online for the cottage I thought it would be ideal to write it in the very house where I was born.' He gives a mock laugh. 'Didn't realise the place was quite so derelict, of course! But once I'm immersed in work, I could be on the moon for all I notice.'

'That's quite a story,' says Jess.

She's not believed a word of it?

Then she adds, 'I'm sorry, I have to dash. Clearing up after the sale of work took longer than planned and I'm expected at a friend's for dinner . . .'

For *dinner*?

'Quick question, Morris. You're a composer. That gives me an idea. Do you play the piano, by any chance?'

'Yes, I . . .'

'I'll text you. Can you give me your number?'

He does, and she gets into her car. They say goodbye.

She is expected for *dinner*? Does that mean . . .?

He continues round to the front of the cottage. A

glance at the sky says it all. Darkness is falling. Lights are coming on in the nearby cottages. So much for sleeping round the clock. So much for not-drinking for two days and two nights. Fuck's sake.

Once inside, he puts the bottle of whisky on the draining board and glares at it. This time it's for the chop. No last-minute reprieves; it's going down the drain and staying there. But first, what fucking day really is it? He takes out his mobile. Battery's gone, of course. He plugs it in.

The Famous Grouse. He murmurs an apology, then starts unscrewing the top.

Laying that trail of breadcrumbs for Jess, what was he hoping for? He is seventy years old, for fuck's sake. He was just chatting with her, not chatting her up. He did leave Majestics, and he really is a composer, and he is working on a commission. Is he so seriously fucked up that even when he tells the truth it feels like he is lying?

Ping. Ping. Ping. Multi-texts from the Accusations.

The day, the date and the time fill the screen: *Saturday 14 March, 7.25 p.m.* So that's that.

Meanwhile, on auto, he begins checking his emails. The usual junk, junk, junk. Until . . .

Another email from McGibbon, sent an hour ago. It is brief. To the point.

Previous email sent in error . . . apologies for any inconvenience . . . your name came up and . . .

Morris struggles to grasp the sense of it.

★

You were at a friend's party when you learned your father had died. Overnight you stopped the aimless wandering, went to college, passed exams, found a good job, did well, got promoted, got married, a house, garden, children.

Meanwhile, you grew to fear seeing him in the room when you woke or when you opened a door, rounded a corner, glanced behind you. You glimpsed his profile in a passing shadow, heard him in a footstep. You kept him at bay with rituals of touching surfaces, repeating words and phrases to yourself. You were casting spells. Your days were an act of exorcism, your nights long moments of terror. Only when you fully engaged with the therapeutic properties of wine and brandy were you able to lay his ghost to rest.

The new millennium was celebrated with a sideways promotion that relocated you to the Edinburgh office that administered biscuits in Scotland. Come the 2008 crash when you watched the news clip of Lehman Bros' employees emerging from the company's multi-storey glasshouse clutching their cardboard boxes, you felt a brief touch of envy. When the crash hit Majestic Biscuits, you were let go. You said your goodbyes and drifted off down the corridor and out into George Street. No box, no baggage. Total liberation. Hip flask recently topped up, you raised it in a farewell toast from the pavement opposite. Downing the last few mouthfuls on the long stroll home.

You walked in the door, told Mary the news and passed out. She was shocked on your behalf and full of sympathy. Tactfully, you kept your sense of relief to yourself. You took to the couch with headphones clamped to your ears, Haydn's complete symphonies and a bottle. Reaching the last of his London series a week later, you switched to Mozart, the piano concertos. You thought you were happy.

Downhill was the only way to go, picking up speed as you went. No commutes, no meetings to attend, no decisions to take. No *anything* to keep you from what you really wanted to do. The days ceased to be a battleground where Drunk Morris and Sober Morris fought each other in your name. The winner had been well and truly declared. Beethoven's quartets, Bach's Passions and Cantatas, Vivaldi's concertos and Scarlatti's sonatas for harpsichord, all five hundred and fifty of them, kept you going through the rest of autumn and the winter. Come spring and better weather you graduated from the sofa to a lounger in the garden. If you felt sociable you took Beethoven, Rossini or whoever for a walk in the park. Two years passed.

Then you came to a decision: your children had left home years ago, and it was high time you left too.

On the morning of your sixtieth birthday you rose early. A clear blue sky promised a fine September day. You showered, dressed, skipped the tea and toast and let yourself out the front door. At the corner, you turned to look back. Though her bedroom curtains were still closed, Mary might already be downstairs reading the letter you had left for her. Did you expect to see her come running up the street after you?

A different scenario occurred to you almost immediately: hearing you leave, Mary had come downstairs, read your note, shrugged and gone back up to bed. And who could blame her? She was better off without you. Everyone was.

Leaving home at sixty is very different from leaving it at sixteen. What had once been youthful hope had long since turned rancid. But, hey, the sun was shining. As a farewell gesture you had given the house, car and everything else to Mary. No more roof repairs to worry about, no council tax, no parking, no MOTs, no nothing. From this moment on, you were travelling light. Striding out of the middle-management estate, you set off into town.

It was a beautiful morning and only the most frivolous clouds had taken to the sky. You raised your early morning hip flask in greeting, told them it was your birthday and toasted them all and yourself in a good long swallow. Coming to the rush-hour snarl-and-roar of the Cameron Toll intersection, you reviewed your future. Was this the moment to peel off and hit the nearby shopping mall for an all-day breakfast? Your life, your choice.

No, you told yourself firmly. Though the main approach into the city meant an uphill trudge right next to a busy road, there would be no settling for the easy option. You were determined to stay the course and earn the pleasures that awaited you in the city centre.

The B&Bs and private hotels that lined both sides of the street and whose front gardens had been tarmacked for patrons-only parking eventually gave way to cafés, shops, bars, minimarkets, restaurants, crowded pavements and non-stop traffic. Edinburgh is not large, and eight o'clock was chiming from the bells of the Tron steeple as you came in sight of the Royal Mile. Here was the simple life: grit, grime, traffic, beggars, tourists, rough sleepers and everyone's indifference to everybody else, and all of it crammed into a no-man's land of pubs, budget hotels, fast-food outlets, tartan tat and Poundstretchers. At sixty there is no Middle Earth, but you had cash and a credit card still far from maxed-out.

Ping. A text. *Good luck. Take care. Mx PS Happy Birthday.*

This was surely the green light. No ties and no responsibilities meant there was nothing to hold you back. In time, a force even stronger than gravity inevitably drags everyone down unless they have someone or something to hold onto. Turning into a fully committed, full-time drunk is suicide in slow motion – call it the scenic route. No rush, not now, not ever, you told yourself as you basked in the sunshine of Princes Street Gardens. Your hip flask was emptied in a toast to Edinburgh Castle, then tossed into a nearby bin. Too fiddly-small for the kind of drinking you were looking forward to. The endless refilling, the risk of spillage – who needed it?

From nine onwards, the Accusations pinged you

every few minutes. Every *ping* hit its target. Mary had sent you her blessing, sort of, but the thirty-somethings were young enough to believe that life's problems came with solutions.

By noon, and already several inches of a new Courvoisier to the good, you decided on a celebratory first-day-of-freedom fish supper followed by a welcome nap in the September sun. That evening you and Courvoisier 2 checked into a budget hotel just off the Royal Mile. The evening passed. So did the night.

Waking early, you stared up at the ceiling. The room was a perfect rectangle with one corner sectioned off for the WC, basin and shower. After an eye-opener from your bedside bottle, you reached for your mobile. It had died, and you had forgotten to bring the charger. Your only luggage was a toothbrush and an iPod's worth of Haydn, Beethoven, Mozart *et al*, plus the charger to keep them hail and hearty. For a moment you felt strangely embarrassed. Embarrassed that these gods of the First Viennese School were witnesses to your . . .

A bad moment, but it passed. They always do.

Sitting on the edge of the bed, you held on to the mattress while the room dipped and slid around you. No real hangover, but the ninety-degree shift of position had set the floor and walls rippling. You waited it out. Like a captain on the bridge, like your namesake Magellan, you were rounding the Cape in a squall. No nausea at least. Well, not much.

To stay upright and better navigate the day ahead, you needed to take on ballast. A proper meal, not a budget hotel's continental crust. If you managed to keep down a full Scottish breakfast, the day ahead would be yours.

First, a shower. A blast of hot to jump-start the circulation. Bracing yourself, you sent the blood corpuscles surging through the arteries. Then cold, taking your breath away. Hot, then cold. Hot, then cold. Hot-cold, hot-cold, hot-cold until you couldn't tell the difference. A brisk rub, on with yesterday's clothes, pocket your luggage, then out the door to track down that full Scottish. Haydn's Symphony 39 blasted your eardrums and put a spring in your step.

Bacon, sausage, eggs, black pudding, mushrooms, tomato, baked beans, fried bread, toast and a pot of tea having hit the spot, you went for a wander along the Royal Mile. Then into St Giles cathedral and out again, down the Mound, sauntering and sipping the length of Princes Street and back, then onwards and upwards through the Gardens to the Castle itself.

So glorious was the late summer's day that from the Esplanade you could see clear to the Fife hills and take delight in the Firth of Forth shimmering with an almost Mediterranean blue. The scene inspired you to picture yourself ambling along the shore, being braced by sea air filled with the screech of gulls as they wheeled and swooped nearby. All very pleasant and easily enough achieved with a bus ride. You were tempted. But which bus? Which bus stop, and when? Would it be direct, would you need to change buses? Would you have the right coins? Would you need to shell out for a day-saver ticket? Could you pay by card? So many hassles, complications, decisions.

Instead, with your hands resting on the low wall overlooking Princes Street Gardens, you imagined the route you would take to get there on foot. Starting at the West End you would go down Queensferry Road, across the Dean Bridge, then, having skirted the edge of the New Town, you would pass Orchard Brae on your right, then Stewart's Melville College on your left and continue on through Blinkbonny to Blackhall, a long stretch of straight road that would be clogged with never-ending traffic heading west, a right at Quality Street and so on down to Silverknowes where you'd step at long last onto the Cramond shore. You felt exhausted already. Could you really see yourself hoofing it all the way out there? In your dreams.

The view from the Castle Esplanade was surely enough in itself – a life-sized postcard, a holiday snap, a memory to look forward to. Contenting yourself with the immediate here and now, you glanced to your left where black-booted, busby-headed soldiers stood on guard with their rifles; there were stone battlements, turrets, the blue and white Saltire flag – another holiday snap. A busload of Japanese tourists was emptying onto the tarmac. You felt an unexpected urge to rush over, mingle with them and immerse yourself in their birdsong chatter, exchanging smiles and greetings as you welcomed them to this near-perfect day in your life.

You didn't rush anywhere, of course, but stayed put, doing your best to keep breathing in and keep breathing out. Time was, if you made too abrupt a movement, part of the magnificent panorama – the section of wall you were leaning on, for example – would have stuck to your hands and torn like damp paper, taking with it tattered strips of Princes Street Gardens, the New Town and the sky above. Which time was that? Your childhood? Or was it about to happen now?

Out of the corner of your eye you saw that the crowd of tourists had vanished and their tour bus was gone. The day was getting on and you'd been on your feet all morning. You felt ready for a spot of lunch. The One o'Clock Gun boomed just as you entered a bar at the top of the Royal Mile. It was packed.

'Pint?' asked the barman.

Of cognac, you almost replied. Joking, of course. Instead, you pretended you were still making up your mind. 'Courvoisier and . . .' Then adding as though it was an afterthought, ' . . . make it a large one.'

Rain was running down your cheeks, into your eyes and mouth. You were sprawled sideways across a bench in Princes Street Gardens, getting very wet. A real downpour. The path in front of you was deserted. The other benches were deserted. A Haydn minuet hammered in your head. No coat meant that your jacket and jeans were soaked through. And so were you. Grabbing hold of the wooden armrest, you hauled yourself upright. It was late afternoon by the Balmoral Hotel clock.

You and a special chow mein checked back into the budget. A Polish man who looked young enough to still be at school and was polite enough to not-notice your appearance processed your card in silence while you dripped over his reception desk. Top floor, different number, same room. You hung your wet clothes on the radiator and turned up the heating. Aluminium trough placed on the budget's welcome pack to protect your bare knees, you forked up the chicken, prawns, vegetables and noodles while watching the news. The half-eaten trough crumpled up and binned, you watched *The Simpsons*. As it is easier to watch TV than do nothing, you then watched most of *EastEnders*.

At the Royal Oak it was folk night, standing room only. Beards and guitars, for the most part, which suited you perfectly. While the beards sang and played, you remained at the bar working your way through a series of half'n'halfs, tuning in and tuning out as the mood took you, and letting the pub-warmth complete the drying-out process on your clothes. There was a piano at the back of a small stage area, but no one used it. Apart from the guitars, there were a couple of fiddlers and a cheerful man who played two penny whistles at the same time. Most songs had choruses that everybody seemed to know. The piano lid remained closed, probably locked, and during the second break, while the bar was taken over by beards bustling and shouting for service and the till rang and rang, you navigated across and sat yourself down.

The piano wasn't locked. You found yourself picking

out the first few notes of Niel Gow's *Lament*, filling in the bass with lightly touched chords. The beards continued shouting, the till continued ringing, and no one paid any attention as you eased into the music. Soon you were swaying from side to side in time. Not only did you not think you might forget some notes, but you stopped thinking altogether. The piece carried you forward, its sense of sadness and longing deepening with every note, revealing the consolation that lay at its heart. When you finished, your hands remained motionless above the keyboard to let the closing notes settle.

Gradually you became aware once more of where you were, and realised the whole bar had fallen silent. The silence went on for several moments. There was no applause, not at first, but then came a smattering of claps, claps that grew louder and louder. You were getting up to leave when someone called out. 'Man, that said it aa! Said it fer every single yin o us. There's a dram waitin at the bar fer ye. *Sláinte!*'

As you stepped off the small stage, the next act – beard like a torn hedge, guitar and harmonica worn Dylan-style – gave you a nod.

'Nice one.'

There were several drams lined up for you.

By closing time, the rain had stopped and South Bridge glittered wetly in the streetlights. You stepped back just in time to avoid the splash of a double-decker thumping down into a pothole. You felt good, the drams were sitting nicely and—

'Hey, old man!' Coming far too close. Twenty-something. Spiderweb tattoo on his neck, dirty white T-shirt and tracksuit bottoms. 'Gies a pun fer ma bus hame, eh?'

'I'm afraid I don't have—'

'Fuck you, then.' Only inches from your face.

You flinched back, and your hand was still shaking as you pressed for the lift in the budget lobby. Still shaking as you keycarded your room.

Old man? The scorn. The tattoo. The feral look.

You eased yourself down onto the bed. You wanted to remember the Royal Oak, the piano, the people clapping, the lined-up drams . . .

Expecting a fist, you hadn't even tried to shield your face. A defenceless old man.

Yesterday's clothes were still damp. Slick, cold and greasy to the touch like day-old chip wrappings, they would start to smell soon. Maybe they already did. You waited to cross the street. There was an unexpected frailty, a sense of caution, as you made your way past the tourist shops and bars. You slipped through an alley, down the Mound to Princes Street and into M&S. New underwear, new shirt and jeans, a raincoat for the next rainy day. New Courvoisier from the Food Hall and you were good to go. You binned your old clothes on the way out.

Keeping clear of other pedestrians, you wandered to the West End and back, slowing down to a stop at shop windows where you stood and stared in before moving on. Clothes, shoes, a travel agent's, books, a tartan gift shop, and you getting slower and slower. Could you bring yourself to phone Mary and apologise, and ask how she was? Too many apologies over too many years, too many promises and too often. Even if you said that this time you really meant every single word. The sad truth was that you always meant every single word. Maybe you could simply give her an update. Tell her about playing the piano at the Royal Oak and—

Your phone was dead, you remembered now, and you didn't know her mobile number by heart.

The computer game was called *Staying on Top*. Two guys in the Oak said they had been working on it for a year. It was production-ready, except for sound effects. The usual pub talk.

Every moment of every scene needed sound effects. A presentation to a games company was scheduled for the following week. They were computer nerds, not musicians. They had tried their best and failed. They were not scamming him, they were not asking him for money, only his skill set as a music man. They were desperate. They were called Alf and Dave. One had a beard and one didn't. Pub names and pub talk, if you had ever heard it.

Until first thing the following morning, that was, when they called for you at the budget and moved you into the attic box room next to the sloping-roofed games office at the top of Dave's house. You were given a desktop and a bed. Meals to be taken with Dave, his beard and his family. Drink wasn't mentioned. Not once.

The game was straightforward. Players started at the top of a mountain; they struggled against each other, against avalanches, earthquakes, hurricanes, tigers, snakes, sorcerers, monsters real and imaginary. If they fell into the swamp at the bottom of the mountain, they stayed there and were sucked down. Last man standing on the summit was the winner. You thought you could rename it *Staying Sober*, but said nothing.

You worked twenty-four/seven, near enough, creating electronic sounds. When you couldn't sleep, you worked. When you craved a drink, you worked. It was one of the best weeks in your life. The game tanked, but your sound effects were well reviewed. You were asked to do more, and you did. You earned. You bought a small flat in a tenement. The years passed. You stopped going to the Royal Oak. You didn't stop drinking. The invitation to write a few slot machine jingles changed your life. So much shorter and easier. So much quicker. Less money, but enough to keep you afloat in wine and Courvoisier.

*

Standing at the draining board, Morris reads McGibbon's short email several times. He shuts his eyes, counts to three, opens them and reads it again. The message remains the same. Same words, same meaning, same kick in the teeth.

★

One evening, you and Mary had been getting ready to go out for dinner with other biscuit-men and their wives. True to form, you had arrived home late and on the wrong side of a bottle. Instead of rushing to get changed, however, you crossed to stand behind her as she put the finishing touches to her appearance in the dressing-table mirror. You placed your hands on her shoulders, intending to deliver a heartfelt apology. As you talked, your fingers toyed with her jade necklace. Even though you could see that Mary was getting impatient, you kept on talking, making your excuses, your promises. You needed to explain to her how—

Then everything happened too quickly. One moment you could feel the weight of the green stones in your palm, and the next . . .

You got down on your knees.

'Leave them,' she urged. 'We've no time.'

There were so many stones, and you were frantic.

'Leave them, Morris!'

You held up a handful to show her, like an offering. More lay scattered at her feet, more still had rolled under the chair, the dressing table.

'I'll re-thread them,' you called out.

There was no answer. That was when you realised you were alone in the room. You placed the last of the stones on the dressing table and were turning to leave when you saw a few were already rolling back down onto the floor. Which made you shake your head and almost laugh out loud, thinking to yourself that you felt a bit like Sisyphus.

★

Cancelled? His string quartet commission has been *cancelled*? Morris puts down his mobile and reaches for the Grouse. To hell with not-drinking. A good long swallow, then another. After McGibbon's email he is going to swallow and keep on swallowing, and when he's done he'll smash the bottle against the wall.

It's the story of his life, the same fucking story, over and over again. Picking himself up and getting knocked back down. His whole life – up and down, up and down. Like Sisyphus, up and down the same fucking hill and getting nowhere.

Sisyphus? He's not Sisyphus, he is the *fucking boulder*! Only this time the boulder's not rolling back downhill as usual – because it's been shoved right over the fucking edge. It's in free fall.

With more than half the Famous Grouse gone, he's well on course for a long night.

Suits him. It can't be long enough. Fucking McGibbon, fucking commission. Fuck. Fuck. Fuck.

Then he's out the front door, out the gate and into the car. Lights, ignition, and gun the engine. Foot pressed down hard, he's off in a scattering of gravel, aiming for the nearest road to town. Radio blasting at max: *The Rite of Spring.*

Headlights on full, he races up the brae, blurring past cottages, the schoolteacher's house, the farm, the small church. Then hurtles downhill, screeching to a halt at the junction. Road empty. Foot down and full-volume Stravinsky battering out on the off-beat . . . A sudden wrench of the wheel swerves him from the B road into a lane so narrow and potholed it has to be a C, D or E. Call it a Z road – and so ruler-straight it must have been tarmacked by the Romans. The will of the state over nature. Whatever. It's a short cut.

The car bumps and thumps along in the darkness, in and out of potholes. Fourth down to third, down to second, going slower and slower. Tarmac giving way to gravel, then to grass. Walking pace. Keeping to a set of tractor ruts till he's stopped by a barred gate in the headlights. A field in front, fields on every side, and not a fucking road in sight.

Wrong lane, wrong short cut. He opens the gate and drives in, scattering sheep. He clambers out to close the gate behind him, that much country sense still remains. Back into the car and, foot down once more, he roars round the field, headlights sweeping the darkness for another way out. Round and round he goes. Third time round, third time lucky – he spots another gate. Celebratory sip from the bottle, which he's had the good sense to bring with him, then he clambers out, opens the gate and he's on his way.

It takes him a few moments to realise he is driving back along the very same track-cum-Roman road, in and out of the very same potholes. The same tree on his left this time, the same feeding trough now on his right. He keeps going.

The junction. Make it one for the road. Then sip number two. And a third for luck. A good long pull.

'Fuck you, McGibbon!' he yells. 'Fuck you!'

With a screech of tyres he accelerates forward. If he is going to free-fall, he'll free-fall in style – best wine, best brandy, best fillet steak and all the trimmings. Because suddenly he is starving; he's ravenous.

Braking in time for the lights into Lockerbie, he skids to a stop. The main street is dark and deserted, the shops all closed. A bar? There will be people, too many people. People talking, people asking. The lights are changing. Red . . . amber . . .

Straight across, quick slew to the left and . . .

He has arrived at a brightly lit space station orbiting the planet of a far-flung galaxy. Arc lights shine down, creating pools of illumination in a darkness that stretches away to nothingness on all sides. Docking successfully, he takes a double sip to refuel, grabs a ground vehicle and moonwalks through the entrance of shimmering glass.

Morris realises his big mistake the moment he's inside the supermarket: while planning to come here he hadn't factored in the rest of the world. Meaning – other people, and far too many of them. A Saturday night and the place is packed? Wherever he looks, men and women who seem to have grown an extra pair of arms each are grab-grab-grabbing everything in sight. Then grabbing for more. And more. And more. He might have had a quick snifter or two to set him up for coming here, but even he can sense the air of – *tension*, is it? Tension morphing into panic. What's with the heaped trolleys? The empty shelves?

Basics first, he makes for the wines and spirits. No Courvoisier? He settles for a bottle of own-brand vodka. A few sips will help him put the night ahead to sleep. Free-fall with no hard landings. He watches his hand help itself to a second bottle. Okay, always good to have backup. He won't touch it, of course. Then one more, for emergencies. That's two extra bottles he won't touch – which makes him feel twice as good. As he has enough sale-of-work honey and the like to last a lifetime and more, he heads for the checkout.

'Ye want that pasta, or no?' A trolley has bumped into his. The woman points to a packet of tagliatelle. The last on a nearby shelf. 'Ah blame the government fer tellin us there's nae need tae panic – sae fowk dae.' She glances at his trolley. 'Ah'd git stockit-up, if ah wir ye.'

'Mmm . . . yes.' He takes the pasta. Why not? He'll score a jar of Bolognese sauce and . . .

The woman has disappeared round to the next aisle.

The Accusations have kept on at him about a possible lockdown, but with the jingles taking up his days, and Netflix and a bottle his nights, he has been too occupied to follow the news. In the cottage, he's been fully focused on his string quartet – until McGibbon's fucking knee-in-the-groin email, that is. Maybe he needs to get panic-buying, before there's nothing left to buy. Tins, packets, anything that doesn't need a fridge. A trawl round the shelves secures the last two tins of peas and carrots, the last two tins of mackerel, a small bag of potatoes and a jar of instant. Plus a packet of tea, some long-life milk and more tins. No Bolognese sauce left. At the last moment he remembers light bulbs. No light bulbs left. He grabs the last packet of candles.

Back in the car, he keys the ignition and reverses. Straight into a—

Fuck.

There's a yell. He twists round in his seat. No car in sight. Nobody and nothing. But he definitely hit something. Heard it. Felt it. Something solid. And that yell . . .

He gets out of the car and—

His trolley. He pushes it out of the way.

'Morris!'

He looks round to see Merv and Mrs Merv coming towards him.

'Ah gied ye a shout, but . . .'

'Some idiot pushed their trolley right into the back of my . . .' He starts to give an explanation that no one's asked for. Then sees a quick glance pass between them.

Merv's looking in the rear window: 'Stockin up in case o a lockdoun, are ye? Ah heard ye hivnae bocht the place at aa. Whit wis aa thon aboot central heatin?'

'It wasn't me who . . . That was a misunderstanding.' He opens his car door. 'A pity there is no central heating, mind you.' He gets in behind the wheel. 'Log fires might be romantic, but not at my age. Give me thermals and a bottle. Hot water bottle, I mean!' he adds with a laugh.

'Richt.' Another glance flits between the Mervs.

A wave as he drives off. At the exit he sees the pair of them in the rear mirror, staring after him. Merv's scan of his shopping must have registered the three voddies sticking out of their bag like flags on parade. Probably smelt his breath, too.

Time for a goodbye toot of the horn. Cheerful.

Dropping a gear, he slows down for the turn-off to the village and starts to climb. In the beam of his headlamps hedgerows loom up on either side, the familiar Scots pine seeming to jump at him out of the darkness. He will probably wake tomorrow with his head hammer-and-anvilling a full Wagner chorus. *Clang, clang, clang.* A few hours' misery that he can count on.

As he crests the hill, he sees house lights spread below like so many scattered stars and is aware of his hand slipping the gear stick into neutral. Then switching off the engine. His descent into the village has begun.

With the headlights doused, the road and hedgerows disappear as if they had never been. The car is picking up speed. Let it.

In utter silence, he coasts downhill through the darkness, the white wall of his cottage rushing up to meet him. Lifting his hands from the wheel he begins to count:

Five . . . four . . . three . . .

Two . . .

At the very last moment he makes a grab for the steering wheel, hits the lights and stamps hard on the brakes. Skidding to a stop only inches from the wall. Its whiteness glares back at him, stark and blinding.

PART TWO

SUNDAY, MONDAY, TUESDAY, WEDNESDAY

After what you saw happen one morning half a lifetime ago, you have often tried to stop drinking.

You were on a crowded railway platform on your way to begin another day as an executive biscuit-man at Majestics. When the stranger standing next to you asked you the time, you told him, 'Eight twenty-one,' and joked about your biscuit-week being already half-eaten. You gave him a friendly smile.

The last person the man sees is you; the last voice he hears is yours. Then he jumps.

Ever since, having been quite unable to take in what had happened right in front of your eyes, you often find yourself back there on the platform needing to check, to check again and again that it is not you lying mangled under the wheels. Sometimes it feels that for your whole life you have been throwing yourself under an approaching train.

That man's day, week and life came to a halt with an abruptness you still carry inside you like a hidden fracture, a wound that might burst open at any moment.

*

Inch by inch, scrape by scrape, Morris guides the car into safe harbour. He pulls the heavy street doors shut, grabs his cargo from the hold, then steps, sea-legs and all, out of the garage and onto the cement yard. As he stumbles into the cottage, the near-empty Grouse bottle slips from his hand to smash on the kitchen floor. Baptising the binge to come.

Thanks to the Mozart/Da Ponte operas at full volume in his earbuds and vodka bottles Ivan 1, 2 and most of 3 drunk between the acts and during the longer *secco* recitatives, there is no Sunday, no Monday, no Tuesday and not much of Wednesday. Dutifully, Morris texts the Accusations every night to let them know he is safe and well—

Saturday, last thing before blowing out the candle: *Cottage spruced up, shpping done. work started. tird. night-night. Love yo both, Dd*

Sunday: *Figaro twice thru tday all fine nite-nte love u both Dd*

Monday: *Don G and Cosi inspirrring all fne love yp bth Dad*

Tuesday: *Figaro is St Mtthew Ppasssion fr everday Its all in ther all fin lve ubth Dd*

*

Even though your life on the London streets is far behind you and so too are Middle Earth, Majestic Biscuits and ex-wife Mary, sometimes you still wake from a night of hot-and-cold sweats, chills and sudden dreams, to hear your parents through in the kitchen. It is Day One all over again and you open your eyes in time to see your father come into your room, triggering another rush of hot-and-cold sweat. He places a tray in front of you. He is smiling.

From the foot of your bed he urges you to eat and keep up your strength. You are a growing boy, he reminds you, and today is your sixth birthday. Your favourite breakfast, a mug of tea and a fried-egg roll, sits untouched on the tray, going cold. His voice is too-warm and too-friendly as he invites you to dig in. But finally, you do. The egg is delicious, slightly runny just the way you like it; the roll is well-buttered and doughy-soft, which couldn't be better. You take your first bite, then your second. Still unable to believe what's happening, you stir in one, two, three, four spoonfuls of sugar, and sneak him a quick glance. He smiles back at you. The smile stays securely in place. He seems very pleased.

For this birthday miracle, and your father's behaviour is nothing less than miraculous, there can be only one reason: overnight he has changed, and in changing has changed the whole world. From this moment on, everything that happens is going to be wonderful. When he asks if your breakfast tastes good, you tell him, 'Yes, Dad, it's great. Best breakfast ever. Thank you, Dad!' You return his love and kindness with a smile that far outshines all the years of your life so far, then take a hearty gulp of tea.

Seconds later, you vomit up the miraculous change, vomit it all over your tray, your blankets, quilt and bed. Retching painfully, you hear the grin in his voice as he apologises and owns up to 'a moment's inattention' when he must have 'accidentally' put salt instead of sugar in the bowl. 'Easily done,' he adds before leaving you jackknifed-over and still vomiting. For the length of time it took you to stir four spoonfuls of salt into your tea you had believed with the intensity that only a child could in a birthday world of possibilities and hope. It had lasted less than a minute.

*

It is Wednesday evening when Morris hears a knock at the door. He'd been asleep. He ignores it. The knocking gets louder, much louder. It's Merv.

'Ah wis in toon an cam soon as a cud. Whit's wrang, Morris?'

'Nothing's wrong.'

'An emergency, ye said.'

'What?'

'Ye texted me.'

'I never—'

'See? A text. An ye sent it.' The phone is held up. 'See

it?' The kitchen doorway is crammed with Merv's red face, red puffer jacket and anger.

'Sorry. Must have pressed the wrong . . . Easy done with these touchscreens. Really sorry.' Morris shuts the door and locks it. Did he really text the man? He is about to check his mobile when . . . he hesitates.

Occasionally drink would make him have blackouts, deleting whole days from his memory as if they had never happened, like a needle jumping several tracks on vinyl. Like the time he'd been in a biscuit strategy meeting one minute and the next a ticket inspector was shaking him awake on an empty train standing in Cardiff station.

Thanks to Merv turning up at the door, Morris pulls himself out of his four-day, four-bottle nosedive. Ivan 3 is almost finished. He pours some of what's left into the sink. Then stops. Puts down the bottle. Remains there for several moments, not thinking, not anything. Then he pours out the rest. Goodbye and good riddance. He manages a few swallows of water, manages to keep them down, then goes back to bed to think things through.

No quartet commission means no reason to remain in the cottage and, given the last few days, every reason to leave. But before returning to Edinburgh he will put things right. Own up to his lies, and correct them. Own up to the truth. The whole truth. The facts.

Which are?

1. He was a drunk, still is a drunk and always will be a drunk – even if he never touches another drop.

2. Drink really is the most important thing in his life.

3. He doesn't drink to feel drunk, but to feel normal.

4. He did not resign his job to pursue his art – he was sacked for being a drunk.

5. He is not a real composer and has not been commissioned to write a string quartet.

By themselves, of course, facts change nothing. They are only words, no more than tokens in a game he has learned to play so well that what he says instantly becomes what he believes – his very own made-up truth. And so . . . no more words. Starting with Jess, it is time for *action*.

He will go to her house and . . .

But where does she live? On the Sale of Work poster her name was given as Mrs Cairns. That she opened the sale and gave out the special prize means she must be a local bigwig. He reaches for his mobile, now down to three per cent, and manages to google Mrs Cairns and the village. It takes him to the website of Marchmont House, the former laird's house, which he knows is only a couple of miles away. Her name is listed as the—

Fuck. The screen's gone blank. Anyway, she must live there.

Right, start again. He will get up, shower, shave, and go to Marchmont House. By then, of course, it will be dark. She will be surprised to see him standing on her doorstep. She will invite him in. He will have brought her . . . flowers? A jar of honey from the sale of—?

Start again. No more lies, no meaningless gifts. Instead, he will *show* her the truth; he will show her the real *Morris Magellan,* and take her the empty Ivan as proof. Being a penitent, he will walk all the way there.

He showers, shaves, sips some tea, nibbles a few oatcakes. A four-day, full-on bender and there's no skull-in-a-vice hangover? Fine, he'll call himself Mr Lucky – believing in *fair* in this world is no better than believing in fairies. Leaving his mobile plugged in to charge, he puts on his coat and slips Ivan into his pocket. Night is beginning to fall as, his head down for steadier balance and one slow stumble at a time, he sets off to call on Jess.

His luck holds: he doesn't meet anyone. After he has shuffle-stepped past the hall, past the primary school and is clear of the village, he feels a slight breath of wind at his back, encouraging him. He slouches onwards. Taking the turn-off up the steep hill to Marchmont House, he feels the wind taking the turn-off, too, as if to stay with him. Mr Lucky, again. Gust after gust, it strengthens, urging him on. Soon it's like he is being blown up the hill, up and up. He straightens his back, raises his head and starts to pick up the pace. As he comes in sight of the entrance to Marchmont House, a particularly fierce gust carries him right up to the massive gates. Grabbing good hold of the wrought iron to keep from getting blown away, he discovers the gates are locked. Of course they are. No sign of a bell either. Two miles, the road getting darker and darker, and him struggling at every step to stay upright – and he expects to stroll in the front door? That would be far too easy.

The walk has done him good, and so will setting the record straight before saying his final goodbye to the village. He peers into the grounds. A gatehouse to the left. Straight ahead, the drive disappears into the darkness up to the main house. What's he waiting for – a super-strong gust that will lift him clear over the gates and set him down on the front doorstep? If only. The gates are high. Too high? Not tonight they're not. The Ivan jammed firmly into an inside pocket and his coat buttoned up to the chin, he prepares to climb over . . .

A bit of a crash-landing, but he survives. Quick status-check. No bones broken; his coat didn't get ripped on the spikes and the Ivan is still in one piece. So far, so good. He takes a moment to tuck in the shirt, hitch up the jeans, smooth down his hair. Presentation is everything.

Clutching the empty bottle, he has hardly started up towards the big house when he catches sight of a white Golf parked just off the drive. Jess has a white Golf. He crunches up a short gravel path to the gatehouse where light is showing above pulled curtains, probably the sitting room. At the front door he raises his hand to—

Then pauses. Time to rethink: alone in her house out

in the middle of nowhere, with the gates locked and no sound of a car arriving, Jess hears a sudden knock at her door? Does he want to give the woman the fright of her life? He lowers his hand.

And suppose her husband is there, too – she is called *Mrs* Cairns, after all – or a partner she lives with, or maybe she already has a visitor? He listens for voices. A steady *drip-drip-drip* comes from the gutter above. When an owl cries from the nearby woods he feels tempted to put his hands together and blow into the hollow of his palms – not too hard, not too soft – to send a friendly owl-sounding hoot in reply.

Then tells himself to get a grip. Owls, for fuck's sake? *Focus.*

No voices means no visitors. There are no sounds of a radio or TV and no music, so she's probably reading, catching up on her emails, doing a crossword, whatever. He takes a deep breath, stands totally upright, back straight, legs apart in a firm stance. Once again he raises his hand to knock on her—

Brr-brr, brr-brr . . . Her phone is ringing.

'Hello?'

It's someone called Fiona and, by the sound of things, this is not going to be a short call. Lots of *really?*s and *right enough*s. On the upside, it will give him more time to work out what he is going to say.

She has just mentioned someone called Drummond. A man, it seems. A man she doesn't like very much. Doesn't like at all, in fact. Apparently Drummond could cause trouble for her. 'But I'm past caring, Fiona,' she adds. There is a long silence. 'That's very good of you,' says Jess eventually. 'I'm sure it won't come to that.' Then she laughs. 'I hope not, anyway.'

Meanwhile, Morris has been thinking. Was he really planning to show her an empty vodka bottle, saying, *This is me, Jess, the* real *me?* Fuck's sake. She'll take one look and assume he'd drunk it on his way here. He needs to get rid of it. He won't be leaving it on her doorstep, that's for sure. Once already is once too often. Hide it under a bush? Dump it in with her rubbish? Jess being eco-green means looking for her recycle bin, looking for it in the dark. As the phone call is not likely to be ending any time soon, he makes his way round the side of her house . . .

. . . and walks straight into a plastic bin, making it rattle. He steadies it. The right bin? He is about to check when . . . Hold on. Next time she lifts the lid to recycle some glass she will see an empty Ivan staring up at her, and she will *know*. Forget recycling. He returns to the front as Jess rings off. Time's up, and he is still holding the bottle. How the hell is he going to get rid of—?

CRASH!

Fuuuuuck!

He clatters down the steps and makes for the gate, slamming hard into it in the dark, reaching up with both hands to . . . stretch . . . stretch . . . stretch. The gate has grown higher since last time.

Her porch light comes on, her front door opens.

'Is someone out there?'

He edges further into the darkness, pressing himself against the ironwork, holding his breath.

She takes a step forward. 'Is someone there?'

She waits.

Realising she is about to close the door he calls out, 'It's me!'

Taking another step forward, she peers in his direction. 'Morris?'

'I . . . I . . . wanted to see you. I was thinking about you and . . .'

'Are you drunk?'

Like a bucket of cold water it feels.

'Morris, are you drunk?'

At the second cold bucketful he steps into the light. 'I'm not drunk. I've come here to . . .'

'That breaking glass I heard. Was that you?'

'I dropped . . . It was empty . . . I was bringing it to show . . . to tell you the truth.'

'You are drunk.'

'No. I need to tell you. I need to explain that . . .'

'Not like this you don't.' She moves back inside until only her head is visible. 'I'm going to close the door now.'

'But, Jess, please . . .'

'Go home.' The porch light is snapped off. 'Goodnight.' The door is pulled shut and he hears the key turn in the lock.

As he comes to the sawmill turn-off, Morris can make out a tractor and trailer standing at the road end. There's the flare of a match and he glimpses the driver up in his cab – big guy, fair hair, a straggle of beard, denim jacket. He's paused to light a cigarette.

Hitch a lift to the village? He could be home in minutes. After that disaster he needs a tin of something hot, an early bed, then straight back to Edinburgh first thing in the morning.

With an abrupt *putt-putt-putt*, the engine starts up, its headlights come on, the tractor lurches slowly forward, exhaust belching out. Singing now comes from the cab, the empty trailer trundling behind, bouncing to keep time.

Morris has to yell to be heard above what sounds like a very ancient engine. 'Hello there!'

The tractor and trailer shudder to a stop; the driver turns round in his seat. 'Ahoy there!' He strains down to see better. 'Ye the music man whae sleeps on the flair?'

Back at the cottage, after tinned frankfurters, pickled onions and bread, he powers up his mobile.

Ping. Text from Jess, timed an hour ago, while he was still on his way to Marchmont House. It was clearly intended for Composer Morris, the ex-business executive who had given up a respectable career to devote the rest of his life to music.

– *Apologies for the last-minute notice. We are planning a short concert before lockdown to celebrate how international our small village has become, e.g. Javid and his wife who run our small post office will give us Pakistani music and dance; Franz, a*

Swiss web-designer, will demonstrate yodelling. There will be some Japanese koto music and also Burns songs. All very informal. Good chance to meet everyone. Might you please play a short piece on the piano for us? Five to ten mins. You can come as a guest if you feel you'd rather say No. But I hope you will say Yes. People will be so delighted. Jess.

Fuck! Fuck! Fuck! Playing at her concert? No way, not after Morris-the-Drunk turned up at her house breaking bottles and . . . And it would have been really fantastic to play and . . . FUCK!

Hurried texts to Elise and Tom: *Might be coming home sooner than expected. Will keep you posted. Night-night. Love you both, Dad.* He powers down and at once starts feeling strangely and unexpectedly relieved. The daily round of jingles with Deliveroo, Netflix and a bottle every evening is looking better by the moment. Set the bar low enough, he can simply step over it.

THURSDAY

You were eight years old when something utterly new and wonderful happened. Coming in from school one afternoon, you heard music on the radio: not pop music, not a Scottish country-dance band that always had you skipping up and down, singing and clapping your hands in time. This music was like nothing you had heard before. It stopped you in your tracks halfway across the sitting room and held you spellbound. Played on a solo violin, it was slow and very sad, but it didn't make you feel sad. Without knowing why, you felt . . . soothed and comforted.

Every time the sad tune returned it reached deeper into you and, promising to come back, it always did. Hearing the opening notes return, you all but wept with relief. Everything fitted together – finally the solemn tone of the solitary violin went slower, and softer, and darker, and then fell silent. When the music finished, your mother said, 'That was Niel Gow's *Lament for the Death of his Second Wife*. He was Scottish.' What she said meant nothing to you, but that didn't matter.

Afterwards you hurried along the road to play with your friend Andy, who lived just outside the village, and all the way there the music stayed with you, its heart-breaking melody slowing your every step until you turned into the lane leading up to his house.

Do you remember what happened next? How you stood motionless, overwhelmed and quite unable to distinguish between the violin tones still resonating inside you and the muddied tractor ruts at your feet, the grass verge, the hedge, the birdsong in the field beyond, the creak of branches in a nearby tree and the slow drift of clouds in the sky above? The radiant intensity of that moment so filled you that the music inside you and all that you could hear and see and feel around you seemed briefly and miraculously held together as one.

Niel Gow's lament continued haunting you for days, and every time you heard violins on the radio you asked your mother if it was Niel Gow. It never was. Instead, she told you about lots of better-known composers from other countries: Tchaikovsky, Dvořák, Mozart, Beethoven, Bach, Vivaldi . . . Unlike everything else that was happening around you, their music made sense. Here was hope; it came into your life and has never left.

*

His breakfast water coming to the boil, Morris powers up his phone.

Voicemails from both Accusations:

Elise: *Is everything all right – Dad? You're not ill, or anything? Please phone ASAP. Take care. Love and hugs.*

Tom: *You're coming back already, Dad? Is everything all right?*

Quick reply to both: *Leaving now. Everything's fine. Work stuff. Will phone this evening. Love you both, Dad xxx*

He is glad there has been no overnight text from Jess telling him to ignore her previous text and never darken her door again. None needed really. If he turns up to play, the door will be shut in his face, and no words wasted.

En route to Edinburgh he will stop and text her his apologies, saying he is really sorry for disturbing her last night and he hadn't meant to . . . he hadn't meant to – what? Smash an empty vodka bottle on her doorstep? But who cares about any apology and any *what* that comes from him. Composer Morris is history. In fact, he's not even *that* – Composer Morris is a never-was who never will be. He feels bad giving up, but doing anything else would make him feel a whole lot worse. Like staying another day here. The cottage was a house of doom when he was a kid, and it still is.

Text from the estate agent:

– *Can you confirm you have removed yourself from Willowbank? The official lockdown is imminent, i.e. you should leave on or before 22 March. As a gesture of goodwill we shall refund on a pro rata basis.*

– *Thank you. I'm leaving right now.*

Short and to the point. Quick mug of tea to wash down some bread, honey and Coco Pops. Packing takes him all of two minutes: toothbrush and towel, iPod and charger; he rolls up his sleeping bag. His creative rewiring of the electricity meter he'll leave as an anonymous gift to whoever buys the house; his food store, minus teabags, jam, honey, and tins, he'll leave to the mice.

He pulls the door shut, careful not to look round in case Neighbour Merv is out and about, polishing his SUV. It takes him less than five to bring out the car, close the garage doors and get in behind the wheel.

Time for a last-minute check: holdall and coat on the back seat, document case beside him, key in the ignition. He is belted-in, buckled and good to—

Someone's rapping on the window.

Has he suddenly gone deaf? Yes.

Another rap. Louder. He glances up to see Jimmy the Post making winding signs with his hand. He buttons down, and smiles. 'Hi Jimmy.'

'Yer no leavin us, are ye?'

The lie is pure reflex: 'No, just going to the shops.' He tells himself to shut it right there, but doesn't. 'The sale of work was great, but I'm getting low on basics.'

'Lockerbie's yer best bet. The back road through Greenhill.'

'Thanks, Jimmy. Can I get you anything?' Fuck's sake, what's he gone and said that for?

'That's kind o ye, Morris.'

If only Jimmy hadn't appeared. If only the shops hadn't been mentioned. If only his packed holdall wasn't sitting there on the rear seat, in full view. If only, if only – how many *if only*s can one life take before it is no longer your own?

'No problem. What do you fancy? We can sort the money later.' Which still gives him a way out. Once on the motorway he can phone the old man – his number will be online somewhere – and tell him he's sorry but something has come up. He feels bad even thinking about doing this. But wait. What's the big rush? Why *not* go to the shop and bring the old man his stuff? Only a few miles extra. Twenty minutes max. Even better, he can do his own shopping for Edinburgh at the same time. Quieter supermarket, too. Win-win.

'Some tins, Jimmy? Bread? More butter, maybe?' He reaches into his document case, preparing to take down the order.

The old man has said something, but Morris is no longer listening. Big block capitals stare back at him from the top sheet of the score pad: *NO ORCHESTRA NEEDED, OPUS 1*. He rips off the page and drops it to the floor.

'Sorry, I missed that. Soup, did you say?'

'Ah'm sayin ah'm fine, thanks. Ma neighbour's gang tae . . .'

'If you're okay then . . .' For a moment, it seems that Morris is no longer in the car and Jimmy is no longer at his window, and the nearby houses, hedgerows, telegraph poles and fields are losing substance, losing whatever gravity it is that holds the scene together. Since pretending he was on his way to go shopping, a gap has been opening up around him, a gap that's getting wider and wider, like when he was chiselling a floorboard. Nothing seems within reach any more, nothing to hold on to, nothing to—

'See you later, Morris.' At Jimmy's commonplace words, the gap abruptly closes and the everyday world snaps back into place.

Morris gives a nod, starts the car and drives off. In the rear mirror he can see the old man gazing up the hill after him, like his mum had done all those years ago. He imagines the relief it would be to shed tears, to let it all go. Whatever *it* is.

Next moment, as he passes the familiar landmarks – the schoolmaster's house, Langside farm, the church – he must have begun shedding tears without realising it. Because everything beyond his windscreen now seems to be draining of colour, to be fading. Hedgerows are slipping out of focus, and the tree he sat under all those years ago to have his breakfast has become no more than an unfinished sketch . . .

He lifts a hand from the wheel and touches his cheek. Bone-dry. Quickly rubs his eye. No tears, nothing. He senses that same gap opening up around him once again and the car losing speed. Slower and slower it goes until it comes to a complete stop. He can't seem to go forward, can't go back. The engine is still running. He switches it off.

A couple of miles further and he would have driven through Lochmaben, then taken the Templand Road, cut across to the M74, turned off at Moffat and climbed into the clouds as he neared the Devil's Beef Tub, then on through Broughton before putting his foot down all the way to Edinburgh. Two hours at most. Instead, sitting motionless behind the wheel, he can only stare out at the grass verge and ditch lining the road, at the nearby hedges and fields. Everything looks normal once more. The countryside is going nowhere, nor is he. Two hours? He couldn't make Edinburgh in two years. Edinburgh is in the future, a future no longer within his reach.

A sudden *thud* on the car roof makes him jerk in his seat. There's another *thud,* then another, a rush of *thud-thud-thuds* that within seconds turns into heavy rain drumming full force above his head, streaming down the windscreen. The shock kickstarts him to key the ignition and ease off the handbrake. The car moves forward. Whatever had him in its grip has loosened and is replaced by a sense that everything in the world is still possible, that he will soon—

The car stops dead. Then lurches down to the left. A pen slides across the dashboard to fall clattering to the floor. His side is now a good foot higher than the passenger side and only his seat belt holds him in place. He clicks himself free, opens the door and . . .

As he stands there in the driving rain, his first thought is loud and clear: he should have put on his coat before getting out. His second thought is a complete blank: he is quite unable to take in what's right in front of him.

Too fucking right he can't.

Then he does.

'Fuck! Fuck! FUCK!' His car is in the ditch.

Feet spread apart for maximum purchase, shoulder pressed against the boot, he leans forward to try and push the car out. He tries and tries and tries. Then straightens up, catches his breath, and tries again. He goes round to the front.

Panting now, he rests against the bonnet to gather all his strength. Having wiped the rainwater out of his eyes, he squares his shoulders, bends down, grabs the front bumper and tries to lift the car out.

'FUCK! and FUCK! and FUCK!'

Soaked through, he gets back inside. He establishes there is no mobile signal. Not in the car, and – he clambers out again – not anywhere within drenching distance. Forget calling a local garage or the AA. Forget Netflix, a bottle and a special chow mein.

Ten minutes later, his coat on, document case in one hand and holdall over one shoulder, he begins the trek back to the cottage, passing the tree, the church, the farm. Just as he comes up to the schoolmaster's house he hears a *ping* from his phone. That's the signal back on and most likely delivering a goodbye-and-good-riddance text from Jess. He continues downhill into the village. The garden gate screeches 'Back already?' as he pushes it open. He tramps round to the front, his door key out, ready to—

On the doorstep stands a small box, shoebox-size, rainwater pooling on its lid and sluicing down the sides. The cardboard is so sodden it has begun to sag. Someone has sent him a package?

Door pushed open, he picks up the box, two kilos at most, the base threatening to give way. He dumps it on the kitchen floor. One glance tells him it's not for him. The ink has run on the handwritten address label. *Willo . . . Willowbank*, the name of the cottage. *YukiTomoko Something* in clumsy capitals. The rest is a smeary blot. The postmark's blurred. The package has come from Tokyo?

By now he should be driving through the Moffat hills, every mile bringing him closer to home – instead, here is Tokyo and YukiTomoko. Nothing's like it should be, not in this cottage, not in this village that he can't seem to get away from – and what a fucking depressing thought that is. If only he—

Just then one of the box's sodden sides collapses and a slew of brightly coloured plastic packages spills out onto the floor.

Morris stares at them, first amazed, then delighted. For a moment all his miseries are forgotten.

Slot machines are reckoned to be the most addictive items of tech ever invented and, whether the punter wins or loses, Morris must craft his sound effects to deliver the one same message – *Put in more cash*. To announce *jackpot*, a truly exceptional jingle is needed to ensure that the joyful cascade of one pound coins goes straight back into the slot machine, not into the punter's pocket and straight out the door. Over the years he has come up with a variety of sound effects to express both the thrill of that moment and the possibility of more thrills and more cash to come. Nothing says it like a rush of electronic whooshes and gurgles. And so, as he gazes down at the unexpected payout that's come from the other side of the world, Morris can't help hearing the ghost of a five-star jackpot jingle.

He looks closer. Several of the plastic packets feature shoals of tiny multi-coloured fish – fish flakes? Was YukiTomoko supposed to eat the whole packet at once? To boil them? Fry them? Eat them as they are? As well as a bundle of plastic chopsticks there are see-through sachets of vacuum-packed mushrooms, dried vegetables and what might be seaweed, exotic tea leaves or who knows what. Everything has been clearly labelled, but in Japanese. There is a handwritten card, also in Japanese, with a picture of birds and tree blossom. As the sender's address is unreadable, the package cannot be returned.

Sorry, YukiTomoko, wherever you are. This is surely a gift from the gods, and not before time.

He takes out his mobile and texts the Accusations to let them know he's decided to stay on a bit longer, adding that he'll call them later.

Next up, Jess's text. This was sent, he notes, at more or less the very same moment his car went into the ditch. Which says it all.

It begins: *Would you . . .?*

Morris stares at the screen in disbelief. Then reads her message again, slowly.

Would you like to play at our concert? Please let me know ASAP. J

Even after last night's disaster, she still wants him to play?

He re-checks when it was sent. No mistake. He reads it again. Still no mistake. Within seconds, a new and much improved Morris, now living in a new and much improved world, replies:

– *Yes. Of course I will. Thank you for asking me. Will be a pleasure. So very sorry about last night. Really.*

– *Not the first time I've seen a Scotsman with a drink in him. Forget last night. I have. Would you like to come and try out the piano?*

He hadn't had a drink in him, not so very recent a drink anyway, which was the whole point of his going there, but it's too late for explanations.

– *Yes, please.*

– *Can you come up to Marchmont House tomorrow – say 5 p.m.?*

– *Perfect.* He adds a smiley face.

A minute later, he texts to ask if she'd mind downloading the score of Beethoven's *Moonlight* sonata, Op 27 No. 2, and print out the first movement. He has no printer at the cottage and will need to practise.

The rain is belting down, the roof leaks, the cottage is a rubbish tip, his car is stuck in a ditch, he is soaked to the skin and dying for a drink – his default setting and always will be – but hey, who cares? He wants to cheer out loud. His life is a slot machine the gods have finally rigged to hit the jackpot at every pull. Time to get into dry clothes, put on a fire and have a celebratory lunch of fish flakes and seaweed.

Having *squelched* through to the bathroom for a hot

shower, he stands on the bare joists, whistling *Ode to Joy* as he towels his hair and face. While adding his own stream to the endless trickle that runs into the toilet bowl, he comes to a decision.

Being all-powerful, the gods are too fickle to be relied on – from now on, *he's* going to be the one pulling at life's slot machine, and all the jackpots will be *his*. He doesn't need anyone's fucking *com*mission or *per*mission to write real music. He came here to write a string quartet and *that* is exactly what he's going to do. Schubert earned very little from his work; he composed because he wanted to, because he thought it was worth doing – and what better reason can there be?

Back in the sitting room, Morris chisels and stomps half a floorboard into grate-friendly lengths. Putting the fish flakes and seaweed on hold until he has worked out how to cook them, he sticks the shiny packets into the bucket then slips two eggs into the saucepan. Soft boiled and scooped-out on soldiers toasted in front of a blazing fire. Luxury, or what? His early lunch finished, he texts the estate agent:

– *Change of plan. I'm staying.*

– *Is there a problem?*

– *Thank you. No problem.*

– *But, Mr Magellan, the lockdown. There is no electricity, no furniture, no heating. No anything.*

– *Thank you. I'm fine. Really. Stay safe.*

Putting his phone to one side, he sits down at his worktable and writes NO ORCHESTRA NEEDED, *Opus 1* on the new top sheet of his score pad.

His car might be in a ditch, but when it comes to his life Composer Morris is now firmly in the driving seat, flooring the pedal and roaring forwards into the good times.

FRIDAY

As your mother's sheet music was always slipping off the top of the piano, your father gave her a paperweight to keep the small stack secure. The lump of glacier-green glass fascinated you and, first chance you got, you picked it up. It was surprisingly heavy and you could see what looked like air-bubbles trapped inside. They never moved, not even when you shook the glass. The desire to pass it from hand to hand became irresistible, and you started tossing it into the air to catch. Soon you were tossing it a little higher, then higher still. You tossed it, clapped once, and caught it. You tossed it, clapped twice, and caught it. Could you manage three? It took all your willpower to stop at three, replace the paperweight on the piano lid and go outside to play.

One afternoon you came home from school to find your mother seated at the keyboard, belting out a Schubert waltz. Seeing you, she called out One, Two, Three . . . One, Two, Three . . . and, taking your cue, you began to whirlwind yourself around the room, shouting out One, Two, Three . . . One, Two, Three . . . back to her. The faster she played, the faster you whirlwinded and the louder the two of you called out to each other.

'One more time, Morris!'

You whirled extra-hard and next moment were sent spinning so wildly you lost your balance and crashed to the floor. Your father stood in the doorway.

'That piano's going to the dump!'

Your mother started to cry. 'Piano goes, I go.'

Getting to your feet, you stumbled dizzily across the room and grabbed her hand. 'No! No!'

'Next time, I'll take an axe to it.' He strode across and smashed his fist down on the keyboard. The discord hung jagged in the air. On bad days you can still hear it.

For weeks afterwards, you ran home from school afraid to find only a heap of smashed wood, tangled strings, black and white keys scattered everywhere, and your mother gone. One day, out of the sheer relief at finding the piano unharmed and still in its accustomed place, you used both hands to strike the loudest two-handed C major chord ever. What a sound! It was glorious, booming out through the whole cottage, making everywhere safe.

Too late you saw the glass paperweight teeter on its stack of music . . . then . . .

CRASH! It lay shattered at your feet.

You fell to your knees and began frantically gathering up the shards. So many, so razor-sharp and scattered everywhere – under the armchairs, your mother's small table, along the edges of the skirting board. The more you picked up, the more seemed to remain on the floor. You were still on your knees when you heard someone come in the door. You looked up to see your father towering over you, and knew that you would never manage to pick them all up, not if you remained on your knees for the rest of your life.

*

Showered, shaved and sober, Composer Morris passes in through the gates of Marchmont House. He reminds himself he is a creative artist who has spent most of yesterday and today working on his new string quartet before dropping in at the concert venue to check out the piano he will play. He also wants to see Jess, of course. The weather is glorious, the country air clean and springlike, and the walk up here has been invigorating. Rhododendron bushes to his left, daffodils to his right, he strides up the drive towards the large Queen Anne house.

The concert will be most likely held in the main hall or in some kind of reception room, which recalls Beethoven at the beginning of his career, playing in the aristocratic salons of Vienna. Like the great man himself, who scorned all pretensions of wealth, class and privilege, he too has skipped the powdered wig and courtly dress in favour of his cleanest shirt and freshest jeans. A pair of stone lions are on duty at the top of a short flight of stone steps, guarding the entrance. Composer Morris gives one of them a friendly pat and . . . *Fuck!*

What a really fucking stupid thing to do. His fingers are now coated in green slime and he'll soon be playing Jess's piano, not to mention shaking hands with her when they meet. Hurriedly, he moves onto some grass and gets down on his hunkers to try wiping off the sticky mess. He wipes and wipes. Its stickiness begins to fade but the green smear only gets larger, greener and smearier. He spits on it and wipes harder, and is still down on his hunkers when he hears the door open.

'There you are, Morris!' Jess is standing on the top step, in a yellow summer dress.

'Hello,' he calls up and tries to body-swerve the momentary awkwardness with a joke. 'I gave one of your lions a pat and—'

'He bit you?'

'No.' He holds up his green hand. 'I've been trying to wipe the . . .'

'Plenty soap and water indoors. Thanks for coming, by the way.'

Morris clambers to his feet. Quite automatically, he makes to shake hands . . . only to jerk back at the last moment. 'Sorry. I'll go and . . . wash.' Too late, he remembers to add, 'Thank you again for inviting me.'

The large reception hall is flagstone-floored with a scattering of expensive-looking rugs; the walls are wood-panelled and hung with paintings. A wide staircase leads to the upper floor. Sunlight pours in through the tall windows.

'Wash-hand basin and towel through there.' A door on the left is indicated.

Alone in the small cloakroom, Morris finds an elderly man staring back at him from the mirror above the washbasin, a very nervous elderly man who's trying to scrub green slime off his fingers. One drink and the elderly man would disappear. One drink, and Morris would be able to clean his hands without fumbling the nailbrush, without dropping the soap onto the floor like he has done already, twice.

'Find everything okay?' Jess is right outside the door.

'Fine. Be there in a moment.' His voice sounds unexpectedly normal.

'I'll be in the room opposite.'

Her footsteps fade across the large hall. Squeezing his eyes shut to concentrate, to *focus* as Elise would call it, he hears his daughter's voice telling him: *Ground yourself, Dad.* Well, he is concentrating, focusing and grounding himself for all he's worth.

He opens them.

Elise. Fuck. He'd worked on his quartet until very late last night and completely forgot about phoning her and Tom, as he said he would. He can't call them now; he'll do it later as he walks back to the village.

Avoiding the mirror, he dries his hands and tells himself that Jess has invited him here, that she *wants* him to be here. And how long has it been since anyone, let alone an attractive woman, has wanted him anywhere? It is years since he has met a woman, actually *met*.

Before returning the towel to its brass hook, Morris forces himself to catch the elderly man's gaze in the mirror and hold it for several seconds. He manages, just. So be it. He gives Old Man Morris the thumbs up.

The hall is empty.

'Jess?'

'In here!' Her voice comes from beyond a set of double doors which have been left open.

Morris is about to enter when he suddenly remembers how, many years ago, he and some other village children and grown-ups had been made to stand right here and ordered not to put one foot in the room, not one step. The double doors were then thrown open to reveal about a dozen men and women in evening clothes seated at a candlelit table, their faces turned expectantly. At a *One-two-three-and* . . . from the headmaster, several carols were sung and everyone wished all the nice ladies and gentlemen a Happy Christmas. The choir bowed, the men and women smiled and clapped, and the double doors were firmly closed again. Out in the hall, next to the biggest Christmas tree ever, a table had been laid out with bottled beer for the men, sherry for the women, and lemonade for the children.

While tilting his head back to finish off his third American cream soda, he had happened to glance towards the top of the staircase. There, next to the landing, he glimpsed a small face peering out between the banisters. It was a little girl. Without meaning to, he caught her eye. She stared back at him for several seconds, then abruptly stuck out her tongue. He was so surprised that he looked away; when he looked back, she was gone.

This, he had thought, must be the little girl who lived in the big house, the little girl who didn't go to the village school and was forbidden to play with the village children. She was seen only at church, where she sat in a rigid, Sunday-best silence between her parents in their own special pew, or sometimes when out shopping at Arnott's with her mother. Everyone said her father was a snob, her mother was a snob and she was a little snob. His mother said she felt sorry for the poor girl, driven to and from the shop, to and from the church, and never seen with friends. She was called *Jessica*.

As Morris goes into the room, Jess looks up from dusting the lid of a fine-looking baby grand.

'The piano was my grandfather's,' she calls over. 'He shipped it out to Malaysia where he was in the colonial service, then shipped it all the way back. When he was alive, my husband made sure it was kept in tune. Drummond had people here over Christmas and the piano was played then. It always sounded fine to me, but I'm no expert.'

The centre of the room has been cleared and the dining table and chairs pushed against the wall. There are a few Impressionist-looking paintings, a chandelier whose crystal pendants drip the last of the afternoon sun. French windows look out onto the lawn and grounds. Crossing to the piano, Morris asks, 'Are you Jessica, the little girl who used to live in this house?'

'Yes . . .' A shadow passes across her face.

With the curved sweep of its polished wood, the piano is a truly beautiful instrument. He lifts the lid and presses down a key. The sound is clear, not too bright and edgy. There is no echo.

'I came up here once, I remember now. When I was a kid.'

'Were you one of the carol singers that time?'

He glances across at her. 'You remember?'

'I remember all right. It only happened once and was talked about for days – everyone patting me on the head and telling me how glad they were that *I* knew to wipe my feet when invited into someone's house; that *I* could be expected to arrive on time and not cause Cook to delay dinner.' Jess has come over to stand next to him. 'Worst of all was that they made me feel proud to behave like that. I was a pretty horrible little girl.'

'Well, you've managed to turn out all right!'

'You think?' She laughs. 'Wait till you know me better.'

Don't you remember seeing me, and sticking out your tongue? he wants to ask, but instead stares at the maker's nameplate. 'It's a Bösendorfer.'

Having delivered this snappy one-liner, Composer Morris swivels the piano stool to a comfortable height, then sits down to test-drive a two-handed C major arpeggio followed by a chromatic run up and down the keyboard.

'It's always difficult for me, coming into the house like this,' says Jess as she closes the double doors behind them. 'I resent that I don't live here any more, which is stupid, but I can't help it. I was born here, you know,' she adds as the two of them cross the hall to the front door.

'My husband Cameron's company went under in 2008, and he died the year after. Drummond, a real finance vulture, took over the debts and mortgages on the estate. I thought I was going to be slung out on my ear . . .' She holds the front door open for Morris. '. . . and couldn't believe my luck when he offered to let me stay on in the gatehouse – no rent, just the bills – in return for *keeping an eye on the place*, as he put it.' She follows Morris outside. 'Which has turned out to mean . . .' She pulls the heavy door shut with a slam. '. . . I'm the caretaker/housekeeper/estate manager twenty-four/seven and unpaid.' They pause for a moment at the top of the steps. 'I deal with any workmen, the gardener; I get the place ready when Drummond and his vulture friends come to stay; I see to the catering while they're here and clear up their mess after they've gone. Then there's the bloody shoots . . .'

Just in time, Morris stops himself from telling her about getting paid a pound a day as a beater at the shoots when he was a teenager.

'You should hear them,' Jess continues as they walk down the drive. 'In between slaughtering the poor birds it's non-stop oil talk, gas talk, shares talk. Like the world isn't in crisis?' Without breaking stride, she turns to face him. 'What do these buggers think – that when the plane goes down, business class stays in the air?' There is real anger in her voice. 'Sorry, Morris, once I get started . . .'

'It's great you've got something you really believe in.'

'And you?' She switches to a mock-interviewer's

voice. 'What are the three most important things in *your* life, Mr Magellan?'

Drink. First, second and third. 'Music, I suppose.'

'Not your kids?'

'Them, too, of course! That goes without saying.'

Fuck.

'I hate Drummond for using me, and hate myself for letting it happen.' She laughs. 'I'm trapped in a gilded gatehouse. When you told me about giving up your business career for your music, I was seriously impressed. You've reclaimed your life. I seem to have lost mine.'

'Well, I . . .'

'How's your . . . string quartet, was it? . . . getting on?'

'Starting a piece is always the hardest part. A real sweat, like you wouldn't believe. But I'm beyond that now and it's beginning to take shape.'

'Must be so exciting. I wish I could *do* something, create something.'

They've reached the wrought iron gates. This is his chance to tell her the truth. The facts. He clears his throat and is about to set the record straight when—

She turns to face him. 'You were my inspiration!' She laughs. 'With nothing to look forward to but the Brexit mess getting worse and worse and the lockdown coming up, I was desperate to do something positive – and your telling me about being a composer gave me the concert idea.' She adds, 'You could say the concert's happening thanks to you!'

Fuck. He can't tell her the truth, not now. And not ever.

*

You started at the secondary school in Lockerbie when you turned twelve, which meant escaping from home all day. It also meant cycling there and back, of course. Without gears, your heavy, old-fashioned bike was punishing work, and the long stretch of main road in and out of Lockerbie was a diesel-exhaust hell of oversized lorries and trucks edging you almost onto the grass verge as they thundered past. That said, to be away from your father for a whole day made every choking breath and every laboured push of the pedal worth the effort ten times over.

It was Day One, and scheduled to be the worst Day One ever. Your mother had taken the train to Edinburgh that morning to be with your aunt who was ill, and would be staying there overnight, not returning till tomorrow. Cycling home from school, you peeled off from the main road at the Heck turn-off and immediately slowed down until you were all but cycling backwards. You wanted to delay your return to the cottage for as long as possible. The sun was shining and the slow movement of Chopin's second piano concerto was going round and round in your head, the perfect accompaniment to your slow pedalling and the leisurely *whirr-and-click* of the chain over the cogs. Recently you had been getting into concertos in a big way, loving how the tunes were passed from piano to orchestra and back again, each adding a little something extra every time round. You and Chopin planned to keep cycling for a good couple of hours longer than usual. You planned to have a puncture.

Greenhill was a tiny village, some half-dozen houses at most, no traffic and, Day One or not, you couldn't resist speeding up as always to swerve in and out of its corners in style, leaving the Greenhillers to eat your dust. Out of the village and back among fields and hedgerows again, you braked to walking pace. At the humpbacked bridge you decided to have your puncture. The bike stashed out of sight behind a bush, you went for a walk along the stream. When you returned an hour later, you were in time to see a dragonfly come streaking out from under the bridge in a flash of blue as if signing off on what had been the best part of the day.

On your bike once more, dread took over. You were going to be late, very late. You would get a row for having a puncture; the bike now had mud on its tyres from lying under the bush, and you would get a row for that. Worst of all, you would get a row for simply being *there,* just you and him. Maybe . . . maybe you could say you didn't feel well and ask to go straight to bed? Though you were getting hungry, you would settle for no tea if it meant no *him.* He would probably give you a row for feeling ill – which gave you a laugh, at least. At the foot of the hill into the village you got off and pushed, making the most of a last chance to slow things down. But once you reached the top you couldn't resist freewheeling downhill, all the way to the cottage.

You went in the gate, along the path and put your bike into the storeroom. You had a quick peek into the garage, hoping to find it empty. He might have driven off somewhere; your aunt might have suddenly got better and your mother had no longer needed to go to Edinburgh. Anything was possible.

His car glared out at you.

You pushed the cottage door to go in.

And couldn't.

You turned and turned the handle, and still couldn't. The door was locked.

Locked? It was hardly six o'clock. You knocked – lightly, so you wouldn't get a row for making a noise. Then waited. You knocked again, a little louder. Then louder still.

You moved along to the sitting room window . . . and *there* he was, in his armchair, reading his paper.

Several times you raised your hand to rap on the glass, only to let it drop. He turned to a new page. You steeled yourself, swallowed, then raised your hand to tap clumsily on the pane with your fingertips. He kept on reading. You tapped again, then tapped louder. This time using your knuckles.

'Dad? Dad?' Your voice was little more than a whisper. Gradually you called louder. And louder.

Lowering his paper, he turned to a new page and continued reading. You kept rapping, kept calling, he kept on reading. If you'd rapped any harder you might have broken the glass . . .

You could see him and he could hear you. You didn't understand. You didn't know what to do. Just then he looked up and stared, stared straight at you. For several very long seconds he continued to stare. Then returned to his paper.

Much later. Darkness had fallen and you'd been wandering round and round the garden for hours. You'd just decided to bed down in the abandoned henhouse where there was still plenty of old straw when you noticed the sitting room light go off. Your father would be getting ready for bed. Surely he would come to the door now? Surely he wouldn't leave you out here all night? You rushed across the lawn in time to see the light in the big bedroom come on. With a swift jerk the curtains were pulled. Minutes later, the cottage was in complete darkness.

You waited. And waited. Eventually, when you tried the front door, you found it open.

*

Morris has hardly gone half a mile down the road from Marchmont House when – Elise! Tom! He takes out his phone, presses the 'on' button, touches the screen. Blank. Blank. And it stays blank. Battery's dead. Okay, the moment he's back in the cottage he'll . . .

Meanwhile, heavy black clouds have come sweeping in from nowhere and within minutes the rain is lashing down. No light-hearted early spring shower this, but a belated winter deluge complete with an easterly that howls through the trees. Quickly, he double-folds the Beethoven printout and shifts it to his inside pocket. He knows the piece by heart, but the score will be his safety net.

He'd felt bad after scattering breadcrumbs for Jess to follow that first time outside the village hall, but now he feels a lot worse. The lies he told her have taken on a life of their own and now he's stuck with them. And stuck with feeling bad. Time was when drink washed any bad feelings away and more drink kept them away. Life was as easy as that.

It is a Very Old Man Morris who enters the village at last, soaked to the skin, chilled to the bone and exhausted. The rain has stopped at least.

'Evenin, Morris!' Jimmy the Post is standing on his doorstep.

'Evenin, Jimmy.' He gives a quick wave and keeps going.

'Ye didnae git tae the shops yesterday?'

'What? Sorry, Jimmy, I'm drenched. Need to get home.'

'Ah heard yer car's in the ditch. Wir ye aaricht?'

'Fine thanks.' Nearly there. 'Excuse me, I best get inside.' He stumbles in through the gate, and thank fuck.

A troop of mice glances up from some spilled-open pasta he'd left on the draining board. With a collective flick of their tails they shoot down to the floor and vanish under a skirting board.

Old Man Morris is so shivering-cold the saucepan rattles against the tap as he fills it. He lights the camping stove and keeps his hands as close round the hissing flame as he dares, remaining there until the water comes to the boil. His tea made and covered with a saucer to keep hot, he is about to go through to the bathroom and get dried off when there's a knock at the door.

A visitor? He remains perfectly still. They might go away.

Another knock.

He opens the door, and immediately starts overdoing it.

'Come in, Jimmy.'

'No, thanks. Ah'm no wanting tae trouble ye, Morris. Aboot yer car. Sailor's yer man.'

'Sailor?'

'Ye'd ken him as Wee Bobby Waugh. Been aa roun the warld since, an fetched up a few year past tae move back in wi his auld mum. They look efter yin anither. His tractor'll hae yer motor oot the ditch in nae time. A tenner at maist.'

'Thanks, Jimmy.'

'Ye'll fin him in the last cooncil hoose afore ye git tae the Post Office. But whit'll ye dae fer yer tea the nicht?'

'I was going to . . .'

Jimmy glances round the kitchen. 'Ye've nae cooker, man! Ye've naethin.'

'I can manage, I'm . . .'

'I wis planning on a sausage-an-egg sandwich. Fancy yin?' Before Morris can reply, he adds, 'Ye look fair done in, man. If ye dinnae mind me sayin.'

Standing in his open doorway, shaking with cold and

in clothes so wet they're stuck to him, Old Man Morris feels seventy going on seven hundred.

'A sausage-an-egg sanny aye warks wunners. I'll bring yin owre. Used tae deliver letters, I can dae takeaway!' Jimmy gives a jokey nod. 'Meantime, git some hot tea doun ye, an intae dry claes. Ah'll no be lang.'

SATURDAY MORNING,
VERY EARLY

A few hours later, Morris wakes to darkness, to the silent cottage.

Drip-splat, drip-splat, drip, drip, drip . . . He feels painfully sober, sober and sick, and with no memory of having climbed into his sleeping bag. He remembers walking home through the wind and rain. He remembers feeling guilty after his not-clearing things up with Jess and not-telling her the truth. He remembers Jimmy calling round. He remembers his offer to return with a sandwich. Then nothing. A total blank.

And yet . . . and yet he remembers sitting at the picnic table, his mug of tea gone cold, hands clamped over his ears, holding back tears that threatened to run down his cheeks and never stop. Had he been trying to block out the sound of Jimmy knocking on the door? Or had he just imagined hearing it? Had he been too distressed to get to his feet and let the old man in? Or is it all his imagination?

The moment Jimmy went off, had he *locked* the door against the old man's return? Had he been feeling so bad he wanted to shut out everything, even someone's kindness? He should get up and check if it actually is locked. He will. Soon.

For the next few minutes Morris huddles in his sleeping bag, halfway between dozing and waking, trying, trying, trying to remember, thinking about the Mervs and Jess, and now Jimmy, and how he has managed to fuck up everything with each of them in turn. Not deliberately fuck up, but do something much worse – fuck up simply because of who and what he is, a seventy-year-old fuck-up on legs. Come to that, what the hell is he doing in this rubbish tip of a house, anyway? It might be his long-ago childhood home, but he is no longer a child. He is as grown up as he is going to get. Not a comforting thought.

Through in the kitchen, he can hear the mice ransacking his foodstore. *Bon appétit!*

Five minutes later he checks the door and . . .

Halleluiah! It's not locked. Thank fuck for that!

But . . . he has no memory of letting the old man in with his plate of sandwiches. Maybe Jimmy never came back? Or . . .? But wait . . . If Jimmy *had* brought him a sandwich, there would surely still be an empty plate lying about. Suddenly excited, he glances quickly round the kitchen: no plate in sight – not in the sink or on the draining board. He grabs a candle from his stash in the drawer, lights it and returns to the sitting room. No plate on his worktable, nor the windowsill. Did he make a fire, eat his sandwich and leave the plate by the fender, or maybe on the mantelpiece? Did he eat it in bed, and the plate slipped out of sight down the side of his sleeping bag? He checks. No plate anywhere. He will need to expand the search.

He keeps looking until, candle held aloft like he's some down-on-its-luck Statue of Liberty on skid row, he comes to a halt in the middle of his parents' old bedroom. But he'd never have eaten a sandwich in here, and anyway—

Fuck's sake, what the hell does he think he's doing? Wandering around in the middle of the night, searching a derelict cottage for a dirty plate? If there is a line between sanity and madness . . .

All at once he starts to laugh. Why not cross the line? Going mad would certainly make his life a lot simpler, it might even be a kind of liberation. He'd be free to think whatever he wants, do what he wants, believe what he wants. He could start making up the truth, his own truth, whatever suits him. Assuming Jimmy did appear with a sandwich, maybe he took the empty plate back with him? Maybe he himself took the empty plate back over to Jimmy's afterwards, and said thanks? When you have no memory, you have nothing and you have everything – and no way to tell the difference.

Out of nowhere he remembers when he was small and walking home one night from a local fair. He had won a yellow balloon tied to a very long piece of string. The night was so black and the string so long that his prize soon disappeared from sight, high up in the darkness. The panic as he tugged and tugged, and the relief as the balloon came into view once more.

Now, standing here in the room where he was born, he feels like he's been left holding only empty string.

★

Your mother kept hens. Feeling sorry for them shut up in their windowless henhouse, you crept out one night to set them free. You unfastened their small wooden doorway and stood back, ready to welcome them to freedom. For several long moments nothing happened. You crouched down, stuck your head inside and whispered, *Chook-chook, chook-chook,* same as you did when scattering their feed. You could sense their unease as they stirred in the darkness, the straw rustling, boards creaking as they shifted nervously, bunching closer together. You whispered a few more times, stepped further back.

Blackie the cockerel was first to show himself at the door, jerking his head from side to side as he looked out into the unfamiliar night. *Chook-chook, chook-chook*, you called to him as loudly as you dared and, at long last, he appeared in the doorway. He extended a clawed foot, paused, then took a half-skip to stand completely in the open. He gave you a look that said *What now?* You stretched your arms wide to take in the whole of the garden, then pointed at the sky. Blackie advanced a few yards further. Behind him, one at a time, the hens emerged and began exploring the unaccustomed moonlit garden. Within a few minutes most of them were roosting up in the fruit trees.

Your father went crazy. From behind the safety of

your bedroom curtains you watched him, torch in one hand, unwieldy clothes pole in the other, poke at the birds as they flapped their clipped wings and scuffled onto ever-higher branches. In the morning you owned up to your mother. She started to give you a row but couldn't keep a straight face. Then . . . how she laughed! The two of you regaled each other with highlights of your father's battle, how he no sooner got one hen down than another would flutter back up. He was at it for hours, she said. Your mother never told him what you had done and it feels good to remember that secret victory shared, doesn't it?

*

Knock-knock-knock, knock-knock . . .

Morris gets up to answer the door. But no one's there. Puzzled, he peers into the darkness. Not only is there no one at the door, but there is no door. There is no lawn either, no garden, no newbuild and no SUV over the fence, no fence, no village, no . . .

KNOCK! KNOCK! KNOCK! So loud it shakes the stars in the sky and when he looks down, he sees them lying at his feet like fragments of broken—

KNOCK! KNOCK! KNOCK!

Morris climbs out of bed. It is morning, bright daylight, and he opens the door to find Jess on his front step. She takes in the kitchen at a glance, then him. 'I've brought you a jacket, white shirt and tie to wear at the concert. They should fit.'

'Thank you, Jess, this is really kind of you, and thoughtful, but . . .' He is about to explain that a collar and tie will only inhibit his playing, that he needs to breathe easy and feel relaxed, that he prefers a more casual—

'Please?' She holds out a large carrier bag.

He hesitates.

'Please, Morris.' She means it.

After seeing Jess to her car, he breakfasts on the last of the Coco Pops and a hunk of bread and jam, washed down by tea. Back in the sitting room he collapses onto the padded mass of sleeping bag and pulls his coat over him like a quilt. He wants to play at the concert, he really does. But more than anything, he imagines himself burrowing deep into the floor, heaping the excavated earth and rubble on top until he is so completely covered that no one can even guess he is there.

The original nineteen-fifties brown-and-beige tiled fireplace still dominates the small room. As far back as Morris can remember, its mantelpiece was an altar dedicated to the cult of Day One. Coming home, his father would arrange his personal effects along it like so many holy relics, placing his silver-plated cigarette case and lighter to the left of the jet-black, pseudo-marble clock that always stood dead centre and no one but him was allowed to wind up. *Tick-tick-tick* it went, Day One and Day Two, and never stopping.

As he lies there on top of his sleeping bag, Morris can all too easily imagine his father home after a couple of days away selling. He's come straight into the sitting room, taken a cigarette from the case, lit it, then blown out the smoke as if to signal that Day One has begun once more. He sits there in silence, moving only to lean forward, tap his ash into the fireplace. His cigarette finished, he gets to his feet and comes to stand above the very spot where Morris lies hidden, and glares down at him. *Useless, a waste of space.* Then he spits.

All at once Morris knows that if he does play at the concert, he will be sure to fuck it up. A terrible truth has suddenly hit him, a truth that has been staring him in the face his whole life: what he really wants is to make himself feel bad, to make himself suffer – because that is what will appease his father. Always did and always will.

A quick scan through his life says it all – leaving home to live on the streets, giving up his love of music for a biscuit career and marriage, giving up his career for drink, giving up his marriage for more drink. From the start, he has been on a one-way trip to give himself and everybody near him a bad time, the worst possible. Even when he comes here to compose real music, which is what he has always wanted to do, he has taken every opportunity to fuck things up along the way. Fuck's sake, Jimmy the Post can't even make him a sausage-and-egg sandwich without his turning the man's kindness into a way to make himself feel bad. The concert will be the perfect opportunity to make himself feel really, really, really bad. A cringingly terrible performance of Beethoven's *Moonlight* will turn into seven minutes of hell, and everyone in the audience will get to share in every grisly moment of it. As a bonus, embarrassing Jess in front of the whole village will be the bright red cherry to stick on top of his very public *Gâteau Fuck-up*.

In a sudden fury, Morris throws off his coat and scrambles to his feet. 'To hell with it!' Best thing is to leave now and never come back. He'll text Jess en route about a family emergency and vanish from her life like he's never been. Best for him, best for her and best for everyone.

Then he remembers . . . His car is still stuck in that fucking ditch.

Jimmy suggested Sailor and his tractor. Okay, he will go and look for Sailor and his tractor. Outside, he gives a hail-and-farewell wave to Merv, who is across the fence vacuuming his SUV, and keeps going.

Jimmy has already told him where Sailor lives. Fine. He goes there. But no Sailor at home and no tractor. Instead, he meets Sailor's mother. She remembers him as a boy and wants to talk about the good old days in the village. Morris doesn't, but he has to. Twenty minutes later she tells him that Sailor is along at the school, she thinks. He hurries to the school. No Sailor. Only his trailer, standing in the empty playground next to what looks like a heap of broken pipes. He is about to leave when a man comes over from the house opposite to say he saw him winning the whisky at the sale of work and asks how the fishing is going and about his staying at the cottage – they aren't charging him rent, are they?

The man knows Sailor. He says everyone knows Sailor. Sailor will have his car out of the ditch in no time.

Sailor, Sailor . . . By now Morris is almost screaming. Forget Sailor. He'll go back to the cottage and google local garages. Cost an arm and a leg on a Saturday, but at least they'll get him out of here. He turns to go when—

Putt-putt-putt . . .

Sailor calls down, 'Nae problem, Music Man. I need tae drap thae pipe bits aff at Langside fairm, fer thir soakaway, ken. Up by the kirk. Ah'll leave ma trailer there, haul oot yer motor an tow it doon tae yer hoose.'

'Will the pipes take long? When can you—?'

'Motor'll be staunin ootside yer hoose in an oor, less mebbe. Nae stress. If ah'm delayed ah'll gie ye a hurl up tae Marchmont on the tractor. But ah'll no be.'

Morris gives him a tenner, returns to his cottage. The moment his car appears, he'll be burning rubber. No more excuses, no more anything. As for thinking he could ever write real music . . . He crumples up the pages of *No Orchestra Needed* and throws them into the fireplace. He is exhausted . . . with everything. He slumps onto his sleeping bag to wait for Sailor.

'Yer dad's in there, aaricht.'

Morris opens his eyes to see a shadow pressed up against the window, looking in. He must have fallen asleep again. Another voice, a woman's this time, shocked.

'The place is derelict. My dad can't be—'

Elise! Fuck. He'd not phoned her, and she's—

There are two shadows now, both looking in.

'Seen him gang in, an no seen him cam oot.'

'But he can't be. No one would live in—'

'He's waving tae us.'

Rap, rap, rap on the windowpane. 'Dad! Dad!'

A bit too fast for comfort, Morris rises from the dead and gives another wave. His shoes pulled on, he goes to open the door.

'Dad! Thank goodness!'

Before he has a chance to reply, Elise has thrown her arms round him. 'We've been so worried. You said you would phone and—'

With Merv looking on, he hugs her in return. 'I'm fine, I'm fine.'

'Seen the wumman gettin upset, sae I cam owre an—'

'In you come, Elise.' Morris starts to close the door. 'Thank you, Merv.' Then pushes it shut.

'We'd not heard from you. This was the earliest I could—'

'I'm sorry, Elise. Really sorry. The battery on my phone—'

'Charge it! Now!'

He does, but is careful to leave it powered down. No sense risking a call from Jess about the concert.

The two of them go into the sitting room.

'What a DUMP! Are you sleeping on the floor? What the . . . what the *FUCK* are you doing here, Dad?'

'There's no problem. I'm—'

'Problem is, you don't see the problem. Bathroom?'

He hesitates.

'You do have a bathroom?'

'Of course.' He points. 'Through there and first right. Mind the floor.' The instant she leaves the room he rushes out to the street to check if Sailor has brought back his car. No car in sight. He rushes back inside in time to hear the toilet flush. Okay then, he'll need to stall Elise until the car appears. If she gets even a hint that it's been in a ditch she'll assume he was drunk. Right: he will take her on a tour of the village; he'll tell her about the cows, their splat-trail steaming behind them, being herded along the main street to get milked; he'll point out the blacksmith's smiddy – now a bijou bungalow – where a giant had once hammered his small tricycle back into shape. He'll make it a slow walk in case Sailor takes longer than he promised.

Then back to Edinburgh. He's had a bad night after a bad week, but that's all behind him. Everything is behind him.

His quartet! She's bound to ask. He whips the crumpled sheets out of the grate, shakes off the soot and dumps them onto the picnic table with only seconds to spare.

'Place should be condemned!' His daughter is back and firing from both barrels. 'My clients at the needle exchange live better. Listen Dad: You. Can't. Stay. Here.'

'I'm not.'

'What?'

'I'm not staying. I'm leaving.'

'Thank God!' She gives him a quick hug.

'Just decided this morning.'

'I brought us a wee snack to have before we drive back.'

He starts for the kitchen. 'Thanks, Elise! I was working and forgot all about lunch. Really kind of you to—'

She follows him. 'I'll make some tea, shall I? Where's the kettle?'

'I use a small pan. It's . . . easier.'

Elise rinses out the saucepan, puts it on the camping stove. She touches a nearby wall and watches as flakes of plaster shower to the floor.

'There's no electricity, is there.' This is not a question.

He snaps the light on and off. 'All mod cons.'

'I'm impressed. Where's the tea?'

Removing a slate from the bucket, he demonstrates

his improvised larder. 'Keeps out the mice! Only the one mug, I'm afraid.' He grins. 'It's all yours!'

'I have to ask, Dad. I can smell . . .' She sniffs. 'Are you drinking again?'

He makes sure to look her straight in the eye. 'The day after I arrived, I won a bottle of whisky at the local sale of work raffle.' A pause for dramatic effect. 'It has already been poured down the sink.' He smiles. The easiest answer and, now that he has said it, he clearly remembers standing at the sink, peeling off the tinfoil . . .

Elise says nothing for a moment, then asks, 'Plates? Cutlery?'

Back in the sitting room, she takes two plastic containers out of her canvas tote bag, and hands one to him. 'Yours . . . and mine.'

As the guest, Elise has been given the fork, the mug and the picnic chair. She has brought herself a salad. Seated on his rolled-up sleeping bag, his back against the wall, Morris starts in on a pork pie, tub of yoghurt and a banana on a freshly washed plate from the stack of jumble sale crockery under the sink. Outside, he can see Merv hard at work polishing his SUV to a blacker-than-black shine.

'I'm so glad you'd already decided to leave, Dad.' Elise takes a sip of tea. 'I was dreading an argument.'

'How are the kids doing?' he asks quickly.

'Like all of us, getting more and more scared by global warming and crap politicians doing nothing.' She smiles across at him. 'You'll be back home soon.'

Too right he will. Edinburgh. Deliveroo, Netflix, a bottle and oblivion on the horizon. He can't wait.

'Do they go on these school marches? It's amazing what that young Swedish—'

'Yeah, amazing.' She pauses. 'My kids worry about the planet, and I worry about them.' She looks hard at Morris. 'And I worry about *you*. If I'd known you were living like this . . .'

'When I'm working I don't notice—'

'How is your string quartet coming along?'

'Powering ahead, thank you.' He points to the stack of soot-blackened sheets. 'It's called *No Orchestra Needed* and—'

The look on her face makes everything worthwhile. She raises her mug in a toast. 'When is the world première?'

The lie comes out before he can stop it. 'Date and venue are not fixed yet. You'll be the first to know.'

'Tom and I are so proud of you.'

'Thank you, Elise.' Making sure to catch her eye, he speaks slowly and sincerely. 'That means a lot to me.' And it does. It really does.

'Nice orchid, by the way. Stylish.' She finishes her tea. 'If you're ready, we'll hit the road. You get packed and . . .' She waves her mug in the air. '. . . I'll do the washing-up.' She stands up. 'Let's get you back to civilisation. You'll be in time for a quick dinner at ours.'

'I've been asked to play at a concert. Piano.'

Fuck. Fuck. What the hell did he go and say that for?

'Wow, Dad! You're really on a roll! That's fantastic! Where?'

'What used to be the laird's house, just outside the village.' He goes into far too much detail about the multicultural line-up, the Pakistani dancer and *tabla* player, the Syrian singer, the Swiss yodeller, the Burns songs and . . . and . . .

'. . . And you on the piano! Sounds great! When is it?'

'Today, at five. But I'm not—'

'Christ, Dad, it's nearly five now!'

'I'm not going.'

'What? Why not?'

'I can't. I don't know. I don't know anything any more. Whatever. I won't be missed.' He gets to his feet. 'Better I give you a quick tour of the village, then we can—'

'You *are* drinking again.'

'I'm not, I tell you.'

'Don't you want to play?'

'Well . . .'

'I'll take that as a yes. What will you wear?'

'What?'

'For the concert. You're not performing dressed like a tramp.'

'Clothes are in there.' He points to Jess's carrier bag. 'But I'm not—'

'Yes you are. Now, super-fast – shower, shave and on with the glitter suit. You do the concert, say your goodbyes, then head straight up to Edinburgh.'

'But . . .'

'No buts.' She pushes him and the carrier bag towards the bathroom. 'You need to hurry.'

She is soon knocking on the bathroom door. 'How's it going?'

'I'm hurrying, I'm hurrying!'

Showered, then dressed, then the fastest shave ever.

He returns to find her waiting for him. 'You look years younger, like my dad again. Now, let's go. You're going to be late, but you *are* going to be there. Haven't they phoned you?'

'Phone's been switched off.'

'Bring it. You can call them on the way.'

He grabs the Beethoven printout and his mobile. Front door slammed shut, they are out the house, down the path and out onto the street. Still no car in sight.

'Just remembered. My car's . . . in the garage. By the time I get it out, lock up and . . . I'll be too late and . . .'

'Get in!' Elise points to her small Fiat. 'I'm sure someone'll give you a lift back.'

Out the corner of his eye he catches sight of Sailor and his tractor puttering leisurely down the hill towards the cottage, towing his car.

'Which way?' asks Elise.

'There.' He points straight ahead past the village hall and immediately wishes he hadn't. Fuck's sake, he should have pointed in the opposite direction and then they'd have arrived too late. 'Elise, it's really better that I don't—'

'I'm sorry I won't be able to stay and hear you; I'm on

duty at the exchange this evening. This was just a flying trip to see you were okay.'

They'll be late, but will they be late enough? Meanwhile, his phone has been powering up. *Ping ping ping ping . . .* A slew of texts, the earlier ones from Elise and Tom, the more recent all from Jess. *Where are you? Where are you?* Last few are question marks only.

He texts back. *On my way. With you in 10.*

There is no reply. It's well past five. The concert must have started. Great!

He almost gives a cheer when they meet a timber lorry coming down the narrow road. Elise has to reverse back . . . and back . . . and back, all the way to the sawmill road end. Ten minutes turns into twenty and it is almost quarter to six when she barrels in through the massive gates and up the drive that's lined with parked cars. At the top she brakes hard.

'You'll need to run!'

He insists on giving her a quick hug.

'Thank you so much, Elise. I'm sorry I was such a . . .'

'Get going, *maestro*.'

He hurries up the steps.

'Dinner at ours tomorrow for a debrief, but keep me posted. Break a leg!' she calls after.

The entrance hall is empty. From beyond the double doors he can hear someone reaching the climax of a song. It sounds Arabic, so passionate and full-voiced it might very well be the final item. He hopes so. With luck, he has arrived in perfect time not to take part. To be on the safe side, he about-turns and heads for the small washroom where he'll lie low until he knows the concert is definitely over.

There is a burst of applause. With a metre still to go, he hears the double doors opening behind him. He smartly about-turns once more and sees Jess coming out into the hall.

'Morris! Thank goodness!'

He starts towards her. 'Sorry, Jess, really sorry, there was a big timber lorry and . . .'

'In you come. Perfect timing!' A quick smile. 'You look good.' She leads the way into the reception room. 'Wait here. I'll introduce you, then give you the nod.'

Morris remains at the back of the room. There are about two dozen people sitting in a semicircle, facing the piano. He should have nipped back down the steps the instant Elise was out of sight. He should have gone straight into the washroom. He should have—

The Beethoven sheets are still in his hand? They are. All of them? They are. In the right order? They are. His fingers are ice-cold, his palms so slicked with sweat he has to keep wiping them on his jeans.

Beethoven's *Moonlight*. He has played it a hundred times. He could play it with his eyes shut, play it standing on his head. For a moment he almost laughs out loud picturing his size tens waving in the air . . .

Jess is addressing the audience. She mentions Beethoven.

She will give him the nod. He will walk straight to the piano. He will sit down. The stool has been set at the right height. Unless someone has reset it. Unless he has shrunk.

Focus. Fuck's sake. *Focus.*

His name is mentioned. Jess jokes with the audience about his winning the whisky at the sale of work. They laugh. With everyone in the room stone-cold sober, him most of all, never has an emergency bottle been more sorely needed. But there isn't one. Part of him feels good about this, but most of him doesn't. Too right it doesn't.

The Beethoven sheets are still in the right order? They are.

The audience has fallen silent. Has Jess finished her intro? Has she nodded to him and he missed it? One sip would set him up, a high-octane rush to charge the nerves and sinews from top to toe – he'd be tanking up on rocket fuel.

She's nodding to him. There is applause. He takes a first step forward, aiming straight for the piano.

He gets there.

He sits down, pulls the stool a fraction closer in, places the printout on the rest. The creak of the stool is the only sound in the room. *Useless, useless.* His hands are poised over the keyboard, shaping the opening chord that will . . . *Waste of space.* His hands start shaking. Really shaking. His mouth has gone dry. He swallows. He swallows again. He feels the sweat running under his shirt.

He should take a deep breath. He can hardly breathe. He should wait until he—

By themselves his hands have started to play, but too

soon. His right hand holds the rising melodic figure for the briefest instant too long and . . . a stumbled note. He needs to keep going, needs to keep the beat.

Back on track again . . . Keep going . . . Keep going . . . He glances up at the score. Wrong page, wrong notes. He has forgotten to turn the page. Should he halt in mid-phrase and start again from the beginning? Should he risk reaching up to turn to the next . . .?

Without his meaning to, his eyes have closed and . . . and . . . and instead, his fingers have begun pressing the keys they know need pressed, feeling for the music. Each note, each chord leading to the next. Like when he was small, he remembers suddenly, and stood one winter's morning at his bedroom window, his fingers tracing the transparency of curves and swirls that had appeared overnight on the glass pane. The ice pattern guiding him even as it melted under his touch.

Sudden silence. His fingers have stopped playing. Have they stopped too soon? Did they reach the final chord? Suspended as if by an invisible thread, his hands remain several inches above the keyboard. The silence in the room is like held-in breath . . . and then he feels his shoulders gradually relax, feels them ease . . .

Someone claps. Another joins in, then another. Soon everyone is applauding. The thread is cut, his hands drop to his sides. Without thinking, he gets to his feet and takes a bow. Jess comes towards him, her face shining.

He takes another bow. The audience keeps clapping. He sees Merv and Mrs Merv in the front row, smiling at him as they applaud. Merv gives him the thumbs up.

Jess has kept him a seat beside her. His performance is finished and it went well. He can hardly believe it.

'That was . . . fantastic,' she whispers as he sits down.

His mouth is bone dry. Never has he wanted a drink more. Rocket fuel and then some, it would be lift-off right through the roof. He notices a table of bottles and glasses next to the wall opposite. There is red wine, white wine, some soft drinks. By its shape he recognises a bottle of whisky.

Four young dancers in their formal highland dress have taken up position in front of the piano. This must be the grand finale. Never has he *needed* a drink more. Just one. Nodding in the direction of the dancers, Jess gives him a quick smile. 'You are about to be upstaged, I'm afraid.'

So many handshakes, so many warm smiles and words of congratulation. There is a drink in his hand. Did he pick it up? Did someone give it to him? Jess introduces him to a man who is all whiskers, tartan waistcoat and kilt. Unable to take his eyes off the whisky swirling in his glass, Morris hardly hears Kiltman congratulate him on his playing then tell him that when Beethoven wrote the *Moonlight*, Edinburgh was still considered by many to be the cultural capital of all Europe. Kiltman namechecks David Hume, Adam Smith and James Hutton. 'And Scotland will be great again, if we can get free of Boris and his self-serving cronies down south. They still think we're a wee colony in their empire.'

As Kiltman ploughs on, the glories of the Scottish Enlightenment, the iniquities of Brexit and the need for Scottish Independence become a mere sideshow to the generous measure of whisky Morris cradles in his hand. Glancing politely from Kiltman to Jess and from Jess back to Kiltman, he wonders if one sip . . . just this once . . . would the tiniest *sip-ette* . . .?

Kiltman has proposed a toast. To Scottish Independence? The Enlightenment? Their multicultural village? Morris missed the details but raises the glass to his lips. The heady aroma hits him immediately, returning him to the moment when the Grouse bottle smashed on the kitchen floor. Once again he becomes Sisyphus's boulder held motionless over the abyss, momentarily unsure about *where* he is and *why*. His only certainty is the glass of whisky in his hand; and his anticipation of its taste is the last remaining balancing point in a world about to go into free fall.

'Excuse me.' He walks off in mid-toast to abandon his untouched glass on the serving table and swap it for apple juice. He comes back to find Kiltman has vanished, to be replaced by Mr and Mrs Merv.

'Thon wis gran, Morris. Fair rugged the hairt, so it did. Ye've a rare gift.' Merv clearly means it and Morris is touched by the man's sincerity. Taking in the room as he sips his apple juice he is suddenly, and quite unexpectedly, aware of how very *right* it feels to be here, at a village event, chatting with his neighbours, the Mervs, and with Jess. This is solid ground. This is where he belongs. Then, like a winning line of fruit on a slot machine, the right decisions click into place. No more jingles, no more booze. Time for Plan B. He will sell his flat, buy the cottage and make it his home once more. A home where he will be happy. He can see it all now: he will rise early and work on his string quartet in the mornings; in the afternoons he will do heavy-duty DIY to get the place fixed up. With the surplus he'll make on his flat, he will employ Sailor to help him. Merv will put in central heating. Once lockdown is over, maybe Tom can come down, take a break from his IT stuff. The two of them will work side by side, some father–son bonding. Leaking roof slates will be replaced, he'll get the kitchen sorted, the walls and floors repaired. Replastered and repainted throughout, the cottage will look fantastic.

Then comes a great idea, the greatest ever: *his mother's piano*. At the first opportunity he will slip outside, phone the Edinburgh Piano Shop and arrange to meet their removers at his flat tomorrow morning. Sunday will be charged double-time, but he's willing to pay whatever it takes to have his mother's piano back where it rightfully belongs.

Jess is looking closely at him. Did he say some of that out loud? Surely not. Instead, the post-performance adrenalin has started him babbling about the ice patterns on his bedroom window when he was a small boy. Jess and the Mervs look puzzled. He babbles on: 'Pressing the keys just now seemed like when . . . when . . .' Another hit of apple juice. 'My fingers on the ice . . . Jack Frost . . .' He looks from the Mervs to Jess.

'You see what I mean? It was like that just now . . . with Beethoven.'

There is a moment's silence, then Jess says, 'The piano has never sounded better, so maybe Beethoven really was there!' The others laugh. And a moment later, so does he.

He smiles at her in apology and to say thank you, and tells himself to shut the fuck up. He can manage that, can't he?

'Wi the lockdoon stairtin Monday,' Merv is saying, 'ye'll want tae git in plenty tatties, plenty tins . . .'

On a sudden impulse, Morris clinks Merv's glass. 'Cheers, neighbour!'

The lockdown is supposed to go on for months. Does this mean the DIY stores will be closed for months? He will need paint and lots of it; he will need tools and brushes, plaster, new timber; he'll need wallpaper and paste . . . The list goes on and on. He pictures his mother's piano stranded in that wrecked sitting room for months on end, and him dossing down every night on the bare floorboards. And anyway, what makes him think the Edinburgh Piano Shop will be open at this hour?

Are these the kinds of bright ideas that apple juice comes up with?

Forget returning his mother's piano to the cottage, forget the cottage *period*. Politeness demands he stand here, sip and smile until it is time to go, and so he will. The Mervs will surely give him a lift back to the cottage. Then it's into the car, heater full on and Vivaldi blasting out all the way to Edinburgh. He will work on his quartet there, then a symphony, an opera, who knows. As for thinking he's got any chance with Jess . . . Him? And at his age? Dream on.

Twenty minutes later, people are saying their goodbyes. Jess is at the front door, showing out the last of the audience.

'Thanks again for the Beethoven,' Kiltman calls over as he leaves. Morris gives a wave in acknowledgement, while running through a final checklist of what he'll take with him from the cottage. Tonight he will sleep in his own flat, in his own bed. He moves towards the door.

'Thank you again, Jess, for inviting me to take part. It was a great afternoon.' He makes to hold out his hand.

'You're not leaving, are you, Morris? I thought . . .'

A woman bustles up. 'We're the last yins, Jess. Can the bairns gie ye a haun wi the chairs?'

'Your children were the stars of the show, Kirsty. I've a wee something for them.' Jess reaches for a brightly wrapped present, wishes them safe home, then turns to Morris. 'You weren't going to leave just like that, were you, Morris?'

'Well, I'm . . .'

'Thanks fer the chocolate, Mrs Cairns!' comes a chorus of young voices from outside.

Looking beyond the children, Morris can see the drive that leads down to the ornamental gates and out onto the road to the village. Dusk is falling and he can sense a touch of early spring in the air. Everyone is heading home to their dinner, their Saturday evening. But much as he wants to get going, he feels he can't just dash off.

'The chairs. If you like, Jess, I'll give you a—'

'I'm not talking about the chairs.'

With his car now out of the ditch and waiting for him outside the cottage, he'll be in Edinburgh around nine, sooner even if he puts the foot down. Spare ribs, chow mein special. Celebratory welcome-home glass. Only the one, of course.

'Goodbye, Jess. Thank you for . . . for everything.' He tries to meet her eye. Doesn't manage to. Instead, he steps past her, blurting out, 'My life, my fault.'

'What?' she calls after.

He keeps going. Out the front door, down the steps . . .

'Morris! Wait!'

He starts down the drive. Struggling out of the jacket Jess loaned him, he lays it on the low wall outside the gatehouse, then hurries through the gates and onto the road. Jess is now right behind him.

'WAIT!' She grabs his shirt sleeve, holding on tight. He strains to keep going.

'STOP! STOP! STOP!' Bringing him to a standstill. 'Morris, I don't understand! Why are you—?'

A car comes tearing round the corner – burgundy-red, tinted windows, sleek – and brakes to a halt only a dozen or so yards short of them. Letting go of his sleeve, Jess goes up to it.

The driver jumps out. In his fifties, expensive clothes, expensive tan. He addresses Jess as Mrs Cairns; his voice drops too low for Morris to make out anything else. Jess looks stunned. After a moment she shouts at him, calls him *Drummond*. They face each other – Jess still trying to catch her breath; Drummond calm and in control.

Morris starts to edge past them, then hesitates. Drummond has taken an envelope from his pocket and waves it in Jess's face. At first she ignores it. Then she snatches it, rips it open, stares at the piece of paper. A moment later, she's rushed back through the gates.

'Jess!' Morris hurries after. The car is right behind him, engine revving, front bumper nudging the back of his legs. He wheels round to see Drummond leaning out of his window, making angry get-out-of-the-way gestures. 'Move it!'

Every drink Morris hasn't taken for the last few days fuels what happens next, speeding it up faster than he can keep pace with. Though he can't see much through the darkened windscreen, he imagines the man glaring at him, and glares back in a fury. 'You bastard! You fucking . . . fucking . . .' He pounds his fists on the bonnet. Next, he's reached in the driver's window and grabbed Drummond by his shirt.

Engine racing, the car reverses, dragging Morris along until he loses his footing and goes sprawling in the road. Moments later, he watches the car pass through the gates and disappear up the drive.

He remains stretched out on the tarmac, then pulls himself up onto the grass verge. He sits there shaking, certain he is going to throw up. Gradually, as his heartbeat steadies, his breathing returns to normal and the feeling of sickness passes. He becomes aware of the evening's stillness settling around him. A blackbird is singing nearby and its unbroken melody seems to bind everything into place: the hedges lining the roadside, a patch of daffodils growing wild and the sweep of countryside becoming indistinct in the failing light. Binding together everything, except him. His shirtsleeve hangs torn and, when he touches his face, his hand comes away blood-smeared. He begins picking pieces of grit from a gash on his arm.

It is starting to get dark when Morris hears a familiar *putt-putt-putt* come up the road from the direction of the village. Sitting high in his cab, Sailor appears round the corner.

'Ahoy there, Music Man! Been in the wars, hiv ye?' The tractorman raises his arm in a cheerful salute and without slowing down continues on through the gates. Stiffly, painfully, Morris struggles to his feet. Still a little dazed, he stumbles after.

The tractor and trailer are parked outside the gatehouse. Overwhelmed by a sudden feeling of hopelessness, Morris slumps down on the low wall next to where he'd dumped the jacket and stares out across the gathering darkness. In the distance the lights of the village are coming on. If he could, he would roll up the scene in front of him like a magic carpet and transport Jess and himself to somewhere safe and wonderful. But he can't. Never mind miracles, he can't do anything very much. Except play the piano, make up jingles and drink.

Sailor has unfastened the rear flap of his trailer,

which drops down with a clatter. He calls over, 'Thon dungheap Drummond is pittin Jess oot her ain hoose. The fuckin erse!' Before Morris can respond, Sailor has disappeared into the gatehouse.

Jess has been evicted? Just like that? Morris glares up at Marchmont House where the only sign of life is a light in one of the upstairs rooms. It would have been a lawyer's letter Drummond handed over. Everything signed and sealed, legal and final.

Jess emerges from the gatehouse. 'Morris?' She's carrying a stuffed bin bag and tosses it onto the trailer before coming to sit beside him. '. . . and there's blood all over your . . .' She reaches up to touch the side of his face. 'What happened?'

He tells her.

'You did – what?'

'I really lost it. I just . . .' What the hell *had* he thought he was doing? The blackbird's song begins again and he wishes he could take hold of it, haul himself note by note back onto his feet, and then he would . . . and then he would *what*? He has no idea. 'Sailor says Drummond is throwing you out?'

'I've to be out of the gatehouse by ten tomorrow morning. Anything I leave behind goes to the dump.'

'But . . . he can't!'

'He can. There's no contract. I'm living here only on his grace-and-favour say-so. Knowing him to be mad keen on Brexit, I never asked his permission to use Marchmont House for the concert. Someone must have told him.'

'But where are you going to stay?'

'At a friend's for the moment. She has a spare room.'

'What about all your furniture and—?'

'Furniture's not mine. Drummond took over the lot when he bought the house.'

'Your belongings then?'

'They'll stay in Sailor's trailer for tonight, and I'm phoning around.'

'If you want . . .' The words are out before he knows it. 'There's a storeroom at the cottage. It's empty. You can keep everything there until you know what you're doing.' This is surely the answer to her immediate problem, and to his. It will give him a reason to stay on, a reason to be *somewhere*, at least. Solid ground under his feet, near enough.

'Thank you, Morris, but I . . .'

Seeing her hesitate, he feels the solid ground already starting to crumble. 'As the Mad Hatter said, there's plenty of room,' he adds. If she says no, he'll head straight back to Edinburgh, back to the bottle that will deliver him into the night ahead and let him pass out in comfort, forever more. Amen.

SUNDAY MORNING,
VERY EARLY

Jess's belongings now safe and sound in the storeroom, Morris secures the broken lock with a nail and some wire. It is well after midnight and he should be exhausted after the non-stop day he's had. Instead, never has he felt more wide awake, never been firing on so many cylinders at once. If he were a sixties' rock band after a gig and the cottage his hotel room, he would trash the place – not that anyone would notice the difference. Add to that, he's starving, and ready for a midnight feast. Tinned mackerel, bread and cheese.

Time was when he and Courvoisier would chill out together, *siesta*-ing away the hours in his Majestic biscuit-tin office. Bottle and glass retrieved from the filing cabinet, Walkman and cassettes from the desk, he'd sit in his executive swivel as the afternoon soared heavenwards on Vivaldi's *L'estro armonico* or dissolved into the slow movement of Beethoven's *Hammerklavier,* letting him glimpse eternity. Drink allowed him to reset the hands of the clock; if he reset them often enough, they dropped from the clock face altogether. Whole days, weeks, months and years slipped past like the countryside seen from a slow-moving train. But not any more. With no-drink and an outside chance that Jess might want to clamber onboard, this train is picking up speed!

He has been thinking of her on and off since she waved goodnight at the gatehouse. Correction – cut the *on and off*. He hasn't stopped thinking about her. His late-night trailer ride through the darkness, sitting perched among her boxes and bags, was made even more exhilarating by the non-stop flashbacks: Jess's smile of greeting on the steps of Marchmont House when he'd come to try out the piano; the laughter in her voice as she'd said *Wait till you know me better*; her look of concern as she dabbed the blood from his face.

He has been thinking of drink, too. As always. For almost as long as he can remember, every moment of his life has been a choice between drinking and not-drinking – which is no choice at all. If he doesn't drink, he wants to. If he *does* drink, he still wants to. Since pouring the last drop of Ivan 3 down the sink, he has woken each morning to a raging thirst, a thirst that only gets worse as he ploughs on through the drier-than-dust hours like he's crossing a desert . . .

It might be the middle of the night, but who can sleep? Certainly not him, for thanks to Jess he is now genuinely inspired, ready to pour his heart and soul into a string quartet that will say it all, and then some. He is feeling wired? Then into the music with it. He is falling in love? Into the music with that, too. He can't stop imagining the two of them in bed together? Into the music with that as well – for starters, it will up the *tempo*! Under *No Orchestra Needed Opus 1* he writes *Dedicated to Jess*.

With their mass of near-illegible corrections and revisions, Beethoven's work-in-progress manuscripts were storm scenes of ongoing creativity that the great composer recast and refined until the purity of his inspiration emerged. Mozart's scores were often note-perfect from the start, and it was said he sometimes composed whole symphonies in his head before committing a single note to paper. By contrast, *No Orchestra Needed* is a crumpled, soot-spattered mess. He shakes out the pages again and smooths them flat.

He can feel the spirits of Haydn, Mozart, Beethoven and Schubert hovering round him, clamouring to slip him their best ideas. Pen in one hand, no-drink at his elbow and a floorboard blazing up in the grate, he still cannot stop thinking about Jess. The notes are coming thick and fast, and each one is *Jess*, each chord, key change and accidental, *Jess*. After a whirlwind start, however, his tsunami of creative energy begins losing power, falters briefly before slowing to a hesitant trickle and coming to a stop. He adds a few notes here, takes out a few notes there. Adds some more, takes out some more. His inspiration at a standstill, all he can think of is Jess. He must be in love, in lust, in *something*. Whatever it is, he grins to himself, it sure as hell clogs up the artistic juices. He puts down his pen.

Undoing the wire in the dark takes several minutes, but at last Morris pushes open the storeroom door and snaps on the light. And *there* they are – the plastic bin bags and cardboard boxes containing all that Jess was able to salvage of her belongings. Leaning against the wall are her hoover, an extendable feather duster, a long-handled broom and the aluminium stepladder that had added so much to the trailer's clatter on the way down from the gatehouse. Hardly romantic, but standing here in front of it all, he feels closer to her.

Everything had been done in such a rush that neither he nor Sailor thought to check if the bags were still tied securely and the contents of the boxes still undamaged after their ramshackle trip. Jess had been so pressed for time the boxes weren't taped shut but had their tops folded in on each other. With one of them in particular, she'd asked him to be especially careful. He quickly locates it and, just to make sure, checks that the eight bottles – a Courvoisier that's not been opened, a single malt that's nearly half-full, plus several reds and a couple of whites – are all safe and sound. Excellent. And they're going to stay that way, even his old friend M. Courvoisier. With only the faintest twinge of self-righteousness he closes the box and replaces it against the wall.

Turning to the pile of bin bags, he allows his hand to rest on the top one, feeling the vibes, as they would have said back in Middle Earth. All the things inside this black plastic sack are *hers*. They are parts of her life. Domestic stuff, by the soft feel of it – towels, bed linen, some clothes, perhaps; the next bag suggests more solid items – shoes, small ornaments, CDs, a clock that he can hear ticking. He remembers her going from room to room in the gatehouse with a bag in one hand, tossing in whatever she wanted to keep and, when the bag was full, knotting it and dropping it where she stood. With hardly a pause, she'd rip the next bag off the roll and move on to grab at random a hairbrush, slippers, make-up kit, a favourite cushion. She had no time to plan, no time to think clearly.

It is just as well he is giving the sacks this careful check, for he discovers one with a small rip. Nothing too serious, luckily. Perhaps it got snagged on the trailer. Not wanting to risk her things getting damp or covered in mouse shit and coal dust, he carries the bag over to the light. Perhaps there might be a way to reseal it?

Bending closer to examine the tear, he catches a hint of the scent he remembers her wearing the day they first met . . . and before he knows what he's done he has made the hole larger. Tangled in a handful of hastily snatched scarves, blouses and jerseys is a length of yellow cotton. Could it be the dress she wore when she greeted him at Marchmont House and they'd joked about the lions? Breathing in her scent and closing his eyes, he can see her coming towards him, the hem of her dress swaying as she descends the stone steps. He remembers how she . . .

Fuck's sake. The hole is even bigger now.

He stuffs the dress back into the sack, together with a silk scarf that has come trailing out along with it. He buries the ripped bag in the middle of the pile, switches off the light and leaves.

Woken by his phone, he checks the screen. Had he been Robert Schumann and the call from love-of-his-life Clara, Morris could not have been happier.

'Hi there, Jess, how are—?'

'Frantic. Sorry, Morris. No time to chat. Can you do me one more big, big favour?'

'Of course, Jess. Anything.'

'It's my piano. I don't want that bastard Drummond to—'

'Bring it here.'

'You're sure?' He can hear the relief in her voice.

'Plenty of room, like I said. There's a whole garage sitting empty.'

'Thank you. Thank you so much, Morris.'

'But how will you move a—?'

'It'll have to be after Drummond has gone. Tonight, late, and in secret. I need to call Sailor now. Bye.'

Jess's piano coming here – how wonderful is that! She doesn't play. Does she want to keep it because she knows that *he* does? Hardly, but it is certainly a good sign. A very good sign.

Showered, shaved and breakfasted, he spends what's left of the morning working on the quartet. When he craves a drink, he works harder. When he still craves a drink, he opens all the doors inside the cottage and marches the length of the building through all the rooms, back and forth, back and forth . . . and keeps on marching until he is ready to sit down and work again, and work even harder. After a quick lunch – tin of Scotch broth, tea, biscuits and cheese – he sets out for an inspirational Beethoven-walk. Then it's back to the picnic table, and back to work.

Having made a good start on the first movement, he feels ready to sketch out the second, aiming for something slow and deep that comes from where it really matters. Chopin-esque yet modern, but not too modern. He sits for a few minutes, eyes closed, and allows himself a quick riffle through some of the great string-quartet slow movements: most of Mozart's, Beethoven's, Dvořáks *American*, Schubert's *Death and the Maiden*, Tchaikovsky, Ravel, Bartók – so many others, and all of them unique and near-perfect. What on earth can he add?

Keep it simple. *From the heart to the heart*, like Beethoven said. An *arioso* with a bass line to be shared between the viola and cello, underpinning a melody for the violins, set in E minor to—

There's a rap on the door. Shit!

He'll ignore it. Think the *Cavatina* in Beethoven's Op, 130, so charged with feeling that the notes themselves seem to—

Another rap, slightly louder.

At the third rap Morris throws down his pen and goes to the door.

It is a young man. Japanese? Chinese? Korean? Long dark coat, white shirt and jeans.

'Good day, Mr Magellan. I enjoyed your piano yesterday.'

'Thank you.' A fan, a stalker even? 'Very kind of you.'

'I had to leave after, too soon. Young children. I have come for my package.'

'Package? I'm not sure I—?'

Fuck! The fish flakes, the seaweed and the rest of the Japanese food that's sitting in his bucket.

'Jimmy tells me you have the parcel from my mother. My is house Willow Cottage, your house is Willow—'

'You are YukiTomoko? I am so very sorry, but the rain—'

'I am Yuki. My wife is Tomoko. Jimmy told me—'

'There was so much heavy rain that day and . . . and . . . One moment, please.' Morris retreats, pushing the door to. Making as little noise as he can, he lifts up the bucket and, keeping it behind his back, returns to the door and peers round it. 'One moment, please,' he says again, and again pushes the door to.

Through in the sitting room he pulls the flattened cardboard box from the pile of kindling and tries to force it back into shape. He shoves the plastic packets inside. Reseal it? He has no Sellotape or—

The insulating tape. It's black, but it's the best he can—

But where is it? After rewiring the meter what did he do with the insulating—?

And, *the card*! Where's the bird-and-tree-blossom card? The card from Yuki's mother. Not on the mantelpiece. Not on his table. He didn't burn it, did he? Fuck's sake, no. Please no. But how come Jimmy the Post . . .? For when Jimmy returned with the sandwiches—

YES! Out of nowhere, it's all coming back to him – Jimmy *did* bring sandwiches, he *did* take away the empty plate when he left. And *YES!* The old man had admired the card propped up on the mantelpiece. Jimmy was sitting at the table, him sitting on his sleeping bag, the two of them chatting. He remembers everything now . . . except for what happened to the card.

A polite tap on the door.

Pretend there wasn't a card? What else can he do?

He returns to the door to find Yuki holding up his mother's card. 'Like I said, Mr Magellan, Jimmy—'

Of course! He gave Jimmy the card as a thank you for his kindness. 'I'm sorry, I'm so sorry, Yuki. It was the rain and I didn't know what to – and I didn't know who to—'

'Please, no problem. Jimmy knows that Tomoko and I are the only Japanese people in the village, so he brought me the card and explained everything. You saved my mother's gift from the bad weather. Thank you.' Yuki is smiling at him.

Morris can't believe it. Everything is working out at last, even YukiTomoko, even the mystery of Jimmy and his sandwich! He's on a roll once more, Plan B it is.

Text to Elise and Tom:

– Great to see you yesterday, Elise. Concert went really well. Have made new friends and decided to stay here. It is home. Lockdown will be a chance to upgrade cottage, incl. a guest room! Love you both, Dad xxx

A moment later – *ping*. From Jess:

– Sailor will pick you up this evening at nine. Fingers crossed it doesn't rain. Thanks again so much. Jx

A kiss! Jess added a kiss! The gods are pulling him jackpots, dealing him aces. He returns to work, stopping only for some frankfurters, a tin of peas, rice and no-drink.

Sailor is on time, his face ablaze with excitement. 'Ahoy there, Music Man! Ready tae rock 'n' roll?'

While Morris gets his coat from the sitting room, the tractorman calls through, 'Drummond hung aroun till noon, then shut the place up an pissed aff back tae whaurever he cam frae, an guid riddance.'

Out in the street, he lowers his voice. 'Jess kens a windae that disnae snib. We'll git in easy an wheel her pee-anny oot the french windaes like it's disappeart intae thin air. Naebody'll see naethin, an serve the dungheap richt.' He climbs up into his cab. 'We'll hae tae caa roun fer the rest o oor crew.'

Having swung through the prefabs for Wee Eck Drennan and his brother Samson, they are soon heading out of the village. The trailer has been loaded up with tools, torches, some rope and a large heap of heavy blankets. It is a clear, crisp night with moon enough to see by as the tractor *putt-putts* out of the village. Sailor calls back out of the darkness, 'Aabody hears us, they'll think ah'm oot poachin!'

Morris remembers Wee Eck from his class in primary. He was big enough then and still growing when he saw him last. A great guy, but easy led. Samson was even bigger, and still is. Wee Eck remembers Morris and asks if it's true he sleeps on the floor, *like yin o them yogi men?*

'Me and Yogi Bear, both!' Morris laughs.

Trading jokes with the Drennan brothers from all those years ago feels good and he is certain now that the village is exactly where he belongs. Sitting here on the heap of blankets facing Wee Eck and Big Samson, the trailer rattling through the darkness, he can imagine playing the piano to Jess in the garage. Romantic, or what? Even better, he will make keyboard arrangements of the quartet, *her* quartet, as it progresses day by day. As Clara was for Schumann, Constanze for Mozart, like Beethoven's mysterious 'immortal beloved', Jess will be his inspiration. Maybe when he's got the cottage looking like new, the two of them might . . .

It is well after midnight when they return. No rain, no wind, and apart from the slow and steady *putt-putt-putt* of the tractor, everything in the village is quiet and still, the road deserted and not a house-light showing. Sailor comes to a stop just beyond the cottage, then reverses the trailer up to the garage. Jess, having driven on ahead, is there to greet them.

With the tractor engine switched off, the silence has everyone speaking in whispers.

'Can you pass me down the key, Morris?'

He does so and she opens the garage door.

'I'll take these to lay on the floor.' Handing back the key, she reaches into the trailer and gathers up two of the spare blankets. 'Morris, I'll need into your storeroom to get a few clothes and . . .'

'It's not locked, just some wire on a nail. Go through the garage and out onto the yard. Storeroom's on your right.'

'Thanks.' She gives him a friendly nod and disappears into the garage.

Sailor, meanwhile, has been talking to the Drennan brothers. 'Ye twa can tak her rear end, like a panto horse, an shove her towards us. Doun ye come, Morris. Guid thing the legs ir aaready aff.'

The tailgate is let down and, the Drennans on the trailer and Sailor and Morris standing below, the four of them slide the large, awkwardly-shaped main body containing the keyboard, metal frame and strings to the back end of the trailer.

'Some wecht, eh?' grunts Samson.

'Things aye git heavier!' Wee Eck grunts back.

The Drennans clamber down. The piano is manhandled off the trailer, then carried, one collective slow shuffle-step at a time, into the garage.

'Richt, lads. Easy, mind. Yin . . . twa . . . three . . . an . . .'

The main body now resting on the blankets, Wee Eck

gives an exaggerated sigh of relief and wipes pretend-sweat from his brow.

By the time the piano legs, the lid, score rest and stool have been carried in, Jess has returned, holding a supermarket bag. Morris tries to catch her eye, to give her a smile.

'Yer pee-anny'll live tae tinkle yince mair!' Sailor grins over at her.

'Well done, everyone. Thank you all so much.' She slips the tractorman an envelope. 'I'll be in touch when I've found somewhere permanent to keep it.'

Sailor and the two brothers go off, leaving Morris and Jess alone in the garage. Since coming back from the storeroom, she hasn't glanced at him once. Like him, has she been waiting for this moment? He can feel the tension and wants to go across to her, maybe even put his arm around her and . . .

Instead, looking down at the dismembered piano, he tries for a joke. 'I hope they can put it back together again!'

No response.

He tries again. 'Reminds me of when Beethoven was given a piano. Stone deaf by then, poor man, and the first thing he did was saw off the legs. That way he could play kneeling down, his ear pressed to the floor to hear the vibrations.' He smiles at her, inviting her to smile back.

She doesn't. She looks him straight in the face. 'Morris? I have something to ask you.'

'Yes?' He meets her gaze. She must have found the

ripped bag. He'll say it probably got snagged on the trailer. Perfectly reasonable. And most likely true.

'Did you go through my stuff?'

'What?' He is genuinely shocked, and sounds it. 'Of course not. My goodness, Jess, I wouldn't . . . I wouldn't dream of . . .'

'I'm not asking about dreaming, Morris. I'm asking if you did.'

There is no way she can know. There can't be. 'All I did was check the boxes to make sure nothing had got damaged on the way here.' Suddenly inspired, he adds, 'Nothing missing, is there?'

'I need to know. That was *all* you did?'

'Of course.'

'Then how come my blue silk scarf has coal dust on it?'

'I . . . I . . .' For several seconds his mind is a complete blank. Then he hears himself saying, 'Won't it wash out?'

Her lips seem to tighten; her eyes glare at him. Glare hard.

He tries again. 'Coal dust? I don't know what you mean.'

'Let me spell it out.' Her voice is firm. 'There is coal dust on my scarf.'

Now for his explanation. 'Yes, Jess, I noticed that one of the plastic bags had got ripped, probably on the . . .'

'Yes, Morris, clearly the bag did get ripped. But my scarf was buried deep down inside the bag, nowhere near the rip.'

'Maybe it had . . .'

She raises her hand for silence.

'One last time, Morris. Did. You. Go. Through. My. Stuff?'

He wants to tell her how his longing to be near her drew him into the storeroom. How he stood there, next to her belongings, and felt close to her. How, when he found the rip in the bag, the scent of her perfume had . . . But it all sounds wrong and will come out wrong. He wants to tell her he is writing his string quartet for her, tell her about his plans to renovate the cottage so that the two of them might . . . How can everything that seemed so right end up sounding so very wrong?

'I don't understand,' is the best he can manage.

'Nor do I.' She walks quickly past him and out into the night.

As he fastens the storeroom door, all he can think of is the bottle of single malt and the cognac. In their cardboard box. Only a few feet away from where he is standing. He remains quite motionless, the desire for drink rushing in like an incoming tide. A tide that will carry him out so far that he will never see land again.

Ping. A text: *My belongings will be removed at the earliest date. Take care of yourself. Jess*

He hears her car drive off.

A few moments later he pockets his phone, goes into the cottage. He makes tea and takes it through to the sitting room. Where it goes cold.

LOCKDOWN

Having fallen asleep in his picnic chair, Morris wakes to find he is so stiff with cold he can hardly move. It is still dark outside. A sudden gust sets the window rattling in its frame. Then *slam . . . slam . . . slam . . .*

He hauls himself to his feet, stumbles through to the kitchen and goes outside. At every step he pictures Jess walking out of the garage, out of his life.

He starts unfastening the storeroom door. Lockdown here in the cottage? Day after day, night after night . . . and for how long? Elise said twelve weeks. Forever, near enough. Sisyphus's boulder? Twelve weeks stuck here and he'll have turned into a wrecking ball, with no cottage left standing. Coming here to work on a string quartet that no one wants and no one's going to play, while trying not to drink? It's all been too much. Whether he drinks or doesn't drink, the law of gravity will still hold and he will still keep falling. So he might as well fall with a drink in his hand.

He crosses to Jess's boxes stacked against the wall and goes straight to the one he knows will clink back at him in cheerful greeting. Eight bottles, ready and waiting. *Eenie, meenie, miney, mo . . .*

Never mind it's the middle of the night. Held up to the light, the warm glow of Courvoisier reveals a brighter sun shining here in the storeroom than anywhere else on earth. He rips off the foil, pulls out the cork and raises the bottle in a toast, not to Sisyphus but to the boulder: may it continue to fall and fall, and never hit the—

Useless . . . His father, right on cue.

'Fuck you! Just fuck off and—'

Give me the axe . . . His father, like he has always been and always will be.

'Leave me the fuck alone!'

Give me the . . . His father, as if Morris had never left home, never gone to London, never married, never this and never that, but had remained trapped here. In this same moment. All his fucking life.

'My whole life! My whole fucking—' Morris whirls round. 'You bastard, you . . .' The bottle explodes against the wall, broken glass flying everywhere.

The single malt is next. *Smash!* 'My whole fucking life!'

The red wine . . . *Smash!* White wine . . . *Smash!* Bottle after bottle after bottle . . . *Smash! Smash! Smash!*

In the silence that follows, he looks at the brandy-whisky-wine streaming down the wall, pooling on the flagstone floor. Finally, glass crunching underfoot, he lurches out into the darkness. Lockdown? He has been in lockdown for as long as he can remember. It is who he is.

A few hours later Morris is woken by the *ping* of a text: *Sailor will call at midday to collect my belongings. Piano to be moved at earliest. J*

Midday! Fuck. In twenty minutes! Having stopped only for a rapid-fire pee en route, he hurries into the storeroom. The stench hits him full force. Glass lying everywhere, puddles of spilled booze. He props open the door, rushes Jess's boxes and plastic sacks out into the fresh air to detox. Frantic, he commandeers her broom and sets to. Eight bottles is a lot of glass when it's swept into one jagged heap. With a piece of slate, he shovels the pile into a cement sack he'll dump later into the hole in the bedroom floor.

Trying to brush the brandy-whisky-wine lake towards the door only makes it spread further and smell worse. His food store tipped out and the bucket filled with water, he ties the rag of tea-towel over the end of the broom and tries mopping. The booze smell soon gets to him, dizzying his head, churning his stomach and staggering his legs. Breathe it in too deep and he's mainlining pure alcohol. What's he going to tell Sailor? The truth? That he threw the bottles at the wall because he'd always wanted to take an axe to his father?

He pauses in mid-swab, the deck still heaving up and down and his stomach with it. He starts to gag, drops the mop and dashes outside to dry-heave in full view of the Merv SUV. And worse – in full view of Sailor who has just come round the front of the cottage.

'Ahoy there, Music Man! Sorry ah'm a bit late.' The tractorman comes closer. 'Are ye aaicht?'

'I'm fine. Bit of an accident, needed some air.'

When the two of them enter the storeroom Sailor gives an exaggerated sniff. 'Been pairtyin durin lockdoon? It'll be the jail fer ye!' He laughs.

While the two of them load Jess's bags and boxes onto the trailer, Morris tells how he'd been shifting everything outside ready for uplift when the base of the wines-and-spirits box gave way and all the bottles crashed to the floor. 'The most expensive drink I've never had!' he jokes, handing over a cheque made out to Jess to cover the damage.

'She'll bide at the Fergusson place, jist ootside the village. Mind it?'

'My friend Andy lived there,' says Morris. 'Andy Fergusson?'

'Nae langer wi us, sorry tae say. Nice guy. Holiday hoose these last few year but naw wi lockdoon. It's whaure Jess'll bide fer the summer.' Sailor pauses. 'Ah'll be drappin aff her stuff there this efternin.'

Morris asks about lockdown.

'Cops'll jist turn ye roun an send ye back whaure ye cam frae.' The tractorman gives him a friendly punch on the arm. 'Looks like yer gang tae be stuck here a while yet.'

As the *putt-putt-putt* of Sailor's tractor fades into the distance, the lockdown silence is reclaimed by a chorus line of sparrows hopping on and off the nearby telephone wires, chattering non-stop. The afternoon looks set to be warm. Morris brings out the picnic chair, a mug of tea, some biscuits and a jar of honey. Powers down his mobile. Sits in the sun. Watches a crow circle overhead before it sweeps down to land on the garage roof with a scuffle of wings and a strident *koww-koww*. It gives him the hard stare.

Two hours later he goes indoors, rips up the score of *No Orchestra Needed* and tosses it into the grate, ready for burning. Tonight and every night for the next twelve weeks he'll be a tribe of one, crouched at his lonely campfire.

The Mervs emerge from their newbuild. Carrying a supermarket bag, cool box and tartan picnic rug, they give him a wave and drive off. After a while Morris powers up his mobile. The Accusations have been texting (Tom) and phoning (Elise). He sends them replies.

It's getting on for six o'clock when he goes into the garage, snaps on the light and pulls the door shut. Jess's piano still lies in pieces on the blankets. There's a smell of engine oil, mice and damp. Mostly damp. The roof must leak. One good Scottish downpour and her Bösendorfer will be ruined. It'll need to be covered.

As he kneels down in front of the keyboard, he realises he's doing exactly what Beethoven would have done after sawing off the legs. Perhaps he and the great composer are the only people in the history of music who have ever got down on their knees to play the piano?

He flexes his fingers. Most likely the poor thing will be out of tune after getting jolted up and down on the trailer all the way from the gatehouse. Whatever. Music is always something good to hold on to.

But when he picks out the first few notes of the *Moonlight*—

'Fuck's sake.'

The beginnings of a Bach Prelude, a Debussy *Image*, a blues riff—

'Fuck! FUCK!'

Out of tune? It's out of fucking notes! No matter what he tries to play or how he plays it – slow, fast, loud, soft – all he gets is *clack-clack-clack*, like wooden blocks being knocked together.

He gives the side of the piano a *thump* with his fist, thumps it again. *Clack-clack-clack*. Fuck's sake. He is about to bring both fists slamming down onto the keyboard . . . stops at the very last moment, slumps forward and cradles his head in his arms.

'It's fucked.' He thumps his forehead on the polished wood. 'Fucked.' *Thump*. 'Fucked. Fucked. Fuck—'

There's a knock on the cottage door.

Footsteps. Firm knock on the garage door. It's pushed open.

'Morris?'

Jess stands in the doorway, holding up what looks like the cheque he gave Sailor. 'Thank you for this, but it's my loss, not yours.' She rips the cheque in two.

Morris struggles to his feet.

Outside, she is waiting for him. 'I need to know. Did you go through my stuff? Yes, or No?'

Whatever he says will come out wrong and be wrong. He blurts out, 'The bag was already ripped . . . and your scent . . . I wanted to be near you. I'm sorry, I only meant to—'

'So you *did*!' She walks off.

'I was sacked from Majestics!' He hurries after, shouting loud enough for the whole village to hear. 'Sacked for being a drunk!'

She wheels round. 'I can believe it.'

A screech of the gate, and Jess is gone.

He's lying on top of his sleeping bag, not dozing, not thinking, not . . . anything. The room is in darkness, the fire unlit, his mug of tea gone cold.

Later still, chilled to the bone, he stands up, pulls on his coat. He needs to walk, needs to get warmed up. Not an inspirational stroll before starting work; he has no work. He has no drink. He has nothing, period.

Out the door, out the gate and off through the lockdown village of shut doors and closed curtains. Not a soul about. Streetlamps for company. Tramping up the middle of the empty street, his footsteps echoing back at him. Past Sailor's cottage, past the post office and a few more houses until, before he knows it, he is crossing the bridge that marks the end of the village. Leaning over the parapet, he stares down into the blackness. From below comes the *slap-slap-slap* of water against the stonework and the ripple of unseen currents criss-crossing as the stream eases round in a slow curve before continuing on to flow into the river Annan and beyond to the Solway Firth.

Open country now. Pitch-dark but for the lights of solitary cottages and farmhouses; there are scuttlings and scrabblings from the long grass by the roadside. An owl hoots. There's the barking of a dog.

He finds himself at the start of the lane leading up to the Fergusson place. He can just make out the large barn, the byre and the farmhouse itself. Lights are burning in every room, upstairs and down. Jess's white Golf stands in the yard. He glimpses her at one of the upstairs windows.

Don't do it, he tells himself.

He is aware of the hedges and fields stretching away into the darkness, aware of the next moment, and the next, and the next after that, laid out ahead of him. The moment when he starts up the lane . . . the moment when he crosses the yard . . . when he reaches her door . . . when he raises his hand to knock . . . He is sober, he tells himself, he knows what he is doing. He can always turn back and return to the cottage. He begins hurrying up the lane.

If she opens her door, he will tell her how sorry he is. Sorry for this, sorry for that, sorry for everything.

As he crosses the cobbled yard, he sees a downstairs light go off. He quickens his pace.

He will offer to . . . promise to . . .

Another light has gone off. He stands on her doorstep, his hand raised to—

He hesitates.

And then, before the upstairs lights too are extinguished and the house is in darkness, he quickly turns away and begins walking. This is all he can do now, the best he can do. He will walk and keep walking, one step at a time, walk to greet the rising sun.

ACKNOWLEDGEMENTS

A very big thank you to Margie Aikman and Steve Catterall, who helped my novel see the light of day. Also to Lynda Clark, Richard Mowe, Alison Service, Christian Albuisson, Ruth and Franz Muheim, Marion Foy, Graham Taylor Dey, Marnie Roadburg and Phil Darby, who all helped Regi and me get through the pandemic with meals, films and friendship. Special thanks to my wonderful agent Kathryn Ross, my enthusiastic and patient editor Edward Crossan, and all the team at Polygon. Thanks also to my friends and readers: Andrew Greig, Anthony Pilley, Pam Thomson, Roger Quin, Malcolm McCallum and Donald Howitt for their support and advice.

Most of all, I would like to thank Regi for all her insight, unwavering belief, encouragement and kindness . . . my first reader, my first inspiration and my first in everything.

An early version of the novel's opening pages appeared in *Lost, Looking & Found* (Merchiston Publishing).

The author would like to acknowledge an Open Fund Award from Creative Scotland which allowed him time to write this novel.